The Legacy of Olaf Stapledon

Recent Titles in
Contributions to the Study of Science Fiction and Fantasy
Series Editor: Marshall Tymn

Eros in the Mind's Eye: Sexuality and the Fantastic in Art and Film
Donald Palumbo, editor

Worlds Within Women: Myth and Mythmaking in Fantastic Literature by Women
Thelma J. Shinn

Reflections on the Fantastic: Selected Essays from the Fourth International Conference on the Fantastic in the Arts
Michael R. Collings, editor

Merlin's Daughters: Contemporary Women Writers of Fantasy
Charlotte Spivack

Ellipse of Uncertainty: An Introduction to Postmodern Fantasy
Lance Olsen

Foundations of Science Fiction: A Study in Imagination and Evolution
John J. Pierce

Alien to Femininity: Speculative Fiction and Feminist Theory
Marleen S. Barr

The Fantastic in World Literature and the Arts: Selected Essays from the Fifth International Conference on the Fantastic in the Arts
Donald E. Morse, editor

Great Themes of Science Fiction: A Study in Imagination and Evolution
John J. Pierce

Phoenix from the Ashes: The Literature of the Remade World
Carl B. Yoke, editor

"A Better Country": The Worlds of Religious Fantasy and Science Fiction
Martha C. Sammons

Spectrum of the Fantastic: Selected Essays from the Sixth International Conference on the Fantastic in the Arts
Donald Palumbo, editor

The Way to Ground Zero: The Atomic Bomb in American Science Fiction
Martha A. Bartter

The Legacy of Olaf Stapledon

CRITICAL ESSAYS AND AN UNPUBLISHED MANUSCRIPT

Edited by
Patrick A. McCarthy,
Charles Elkins,
and
Martin Harry Greenberg

Contributions to the Study of Science Fiction and Fantasy,
Number 34

GREENWOOD PRESS
New York • Westport, Connecticut • London

Library of Congress Cataloging-in-Publication Data

The Legacy of Olaf Stapledon : critical essays and an unpublished manuscript / edited by Patrick A. McCarthy, Charles Elkins, and Martin Harry Greenberg.
p. cm. — (Contributions to the study of science fiction and fantasy, ISSN 0193-6875 ; no. 34)
Bibliography: p.
Includes index.
"Olaf Stapledon's 'Letters to the future' edited by Robert Crossley": p.
ISBN 0-313-26114-8 (lib bdg. : alk. paper)
1. Stapledon, Olaf, 1886–1950—Criticism and interpretation. 2. Science fiction, English—History and criticism. I. McCarthy, Patrick A., 1945– . II. Elkins, Charles. III. Greenberg, Martin Harry. IV. Stapledon, Olaf, 1886–1950. Letters to the future. 1989. V. Series.
PR6037.T18Z75 1989
828′.912—dc19 88-25097

British Library Cataloguing in Publication Data is available.

Library of Congress Catalog Card Number: 88-25097
ISBN: 0-313-26114-8
ISSN: 0193-6875

First published in 1989

Greenwood Press, Inc.
88 Post Road West, Westport, Connecticut 06881

Printed in the United States of America

The paper used in this book complies with the Permanent Paper Standard issued by the National Information Standards Organization (Z39.48–1984).

10 9 8 7 6 5 4 3 2 1

Copyright Acknowledgments

For permission to quote, we wish to thank the following people, publishers, and agencies:

The Estate of Olaf Stapledon, for quotations from Stapledon's poem "Revolt Against Death" (in *Poets of Merseyside*, edited by S. Fowler Wright, Merton Press, 1923); from letters by Stapledon published in *Talking Across The World: The Love Letters of Olaf Stapledon and Agnes Miller, 1913–1919*, edited by Robert Crossley (University Press of New England, 1987); from unpublished letters by Stapledon in the collection of John D. Stapledon; and from Stapledon's *A Modern Theory of Ethics* (Methuen, 1929), *Waking World* (Methuen, 1934), *Death into Life* (Methuen, 1946), and *The Opening of the Eyes* (Methuen, 1954).

The Librarian, Sydney Jones Library, University of Liverpool, and the Estate of Olaf Stapledon, for the transcription of Stapledon's "Letters to the Future" and a quotation from Stapledon's "Thoughts on the Modern Spirit."

The Trustees of the National Library of Scotland and Lady Naomi Mitchison, for an extract from a letter of 10 July 1940 from Olaf Stapledon to Lady Mitchison.

Methuen & Co., Ltd., for citations from Olaf Stapledon's *Last Men In London* (Methuen, 1932), *Odd John* (Methuen, 1935), and *Star Maker* (Methuen, 1937).

Secker & Warburg, Ltd., for quotations from Stapledon's *Beyond the "Isms"* (Secker & Warburg, 1942), *Sirius* (Secker & Warburg, 1944), and *The Flames* (Secker & Warburg, 1947).

Penguin Books, Ltd., for citations from Stapledon's *Philosophy and Living* (Penguin Books, 1939). Reproduced by permission of Penguin Books Ltd.

William Heinemann, Ltd., for quotations from Stapledon's *Saints and Revolutionaries* (William Heinemann, 1939). Reprinted by permission of William Heinemann Limited.

The University of California Press, for extracts from Martin Jay's *Marxism and Totality: The Adventures of a Concept from Lukacs to Habermas* (University of California Press, 1984).

Harper & Row, Publishers, Inc., for quotations from Mircea Eliade's *Rites and Symbols of Initiation*, translated by Willard R. Trask (Harper & Row, 1958).

De Gruyter Aldine, for citations from Victor W. Turner's *The Ritual Process* (New York: Aldine, 1969). Copyright © 1969 by Victor W. Turner.

Contents

A Note on Citations

In this collection of essays, Stapledon's novels are referred to parenthetically by chapter and page numbers, his non-fiction books by page numbers alone. Citations are preceded by an identifying abbreviation or short title, as listed below. Here, we give publication information on books for which we have used currently available reprints as our texts; for information on the first editions of these and other books, see the bibliography.

Death	*Death into Life*, 1946. First edition.
DL	*Darkness and the Light*, 1942. Reprint: Westport, Conn.: Hyperion Press, 1974.
Ethics	*A Modern Theory of Ethics*, 1929. First edition.
FE	*Four Encounters*, 1976. Reprint: *"Nebula Maker" & "Four Encounters."* New York: Dodd, Mead & Company, 1983
FFC	*Far Future Calling: Uncollected Science Fiction and Fantasies of Olaf Stapledon*, 1979. First edition.
Flames	*The Flames*, 1947. First edition.
Isms	*Beyond the "Isms,"* 1942. First edition.

LDP	*Latter-Day Psalms*, 1914. First edition.
LFM	*Last and First Men: A Story of the Near and Far Future*, 1930. Reprint: *"Last and First Men" & "Star Maker": Two Science-Fiction Novels.* New York: Dover Publications, 1968.
LML	*Last Men in London*, 1932. Reprint: London: Magnum Books, 1978.
MD	*A Man Divided*, 1950. First edition.
NHB	*New Hope for Britain*, 1939. First edition.
NM	*"Nebula Maker,"* 1976. Reprint: *"Nebula Maker" & "Four Encounters."* New York Dodd, Mead & Company, 1983.
OE	*The Opening of the Eyes*, 1954. First edition.
OJ	*Odd John: A Story between Jest and Earnest*, 1935. Reprint: *"Odd John" & Sirius": Two Science-Fiction Novels.* New York: Dover Publications, 1972.
OM	*Old Man in New World*, 1944. First edition.
PL	*Philosophy and Living*, 1939. First edition.
Sirius	*Sirius: A Fantasy of Love and Discord*, 1944. Reprint: *"Odd John" & "Sirius": Two Science-Fiction Novels.* New York: Dover Publications, 1972.
SR	*Saints and Revolutionaries*, 1939. First edition.
SM	*Star Maker*, 1937. Reprint: *"Last and First Men" & "Star Maker": Two Science-Fiction Novels.* New York: Dover Publications, 1968.
WW	*Waking World*, 1934. First edition.
YT	*Youth and Tomorrow*, 1946. First edition.

The Legacy of Olaf Stapledon

Introduction

Patrick A. McCarthy

Olaf Stapledon's death in 1950 deprived the science fiction community of one of its most original and profound imaginations, for over the previous twenty years Stapledon had published a series of novels whose conceptual scope, narrative innovations, and intellectual audacity remain essentially unparalleled in the field of science fiction. Even so, a combination of factors—Stapledon's geographical isolation from most readers of science fiction, the intellectual tone of his work, the leftist bias discernible in his fiction—conspired to render him a marginal figure in his own field, someone more often respected than read. Despite the publication of an omnibus volume, *To the End of Time: The Best of Olaf Stapledon*, in 1953, and a posthumous visionary work, *The Opening of the Eyes*, the following year, Stapledon drifted into obscurity over the next two decades, a period in which Stapledon's science fiction received virtually no attention from the scholarly community. In the early 1970s, however, a few significant articles began to appear, spurred in part by growing academic and scholarly interest in science fiction generally. The publication in this decade of three critical volumes on Stapledon as well as numerous journal articles (including eight in a special Stapledon issue of *Science-Fiction Studies*) is further evidence of the regeneration of interest in Stapledon.

While most of the criticism of Stapledon's works in recent years has focused either on the themes and narrative strategies of individual novels, or on Stapledon's relationship to various literary antecedents, the essays collected in the present volume reveal a variety of new approaches to Stapledon. The first four essays concern themselves with philosophical, political, and aesthetic issues that recur throughout Stapledon's writings. Robert Shelton focuses on Stapledon's non-fiction in his consideration of the philosophical, political, and religious dimensions of Stapledon's treatment of morality. In so doing, he raises questions that will inevitably affect readings of the science fiction novels. Dealing directly with the science fiction, Cheryl Herr argues that a largely unacknowledged struggle between convention and spirit underlies Stapledon's dichotomies of individualism and community, materialism and spirituality, and prevents a narrative resolution of these issues in the fiction. My own contribution reveals affinities between Stapledon's fiction and that of the major Modernist writers, as well as a more sympathetic, if complex, view of the Modernists than previous critics have noted. Charles Elkins concentrates on *Last and First Men* and *Star Maker*, but his analysis of the problems inherent in Stapledon's attempt to create a vision of totality raises an issue that is crucial not only to Stapledon's fictional writings in general, but also to critical interpretations of the fiction.

The remaining essays open up other new avenues of inquiry. In his discussion of ritual experience in *Odd John* and *Sirius*, Louis Tremaine shows that the books' ritualistic element affects both their moral dimension and their narrative strategies. Curtis C. Smith, one of the pioneers of modern Stapledon criticism, moves outside the established canon to examine an extended exchange of letters in the *Liverpool Daily Post* between Stapledon and an anonymous antagonist who signed himself "Ignotus." In so doing, he sheds light on the difficulties that Stapledon faced in maintaining his pacifist stance during the late 1930s and shows that this debate has a direct relationship to *Star Maker*, the only major piece of fiction that Stapledon wrote during this period. Finally, Stapledon's own essay "Letters to the Future," edited by Robert Crossley and published here for the first time, is a wide-ranging commentary on various aspects of modern civilization, one of Stapledon's most substantial efforts, apart from the major novels, to come to grips with the spiritual crisis he saw in his own civilization.

The first six essays might well have earned this collection the title *Olaf Stapledon in Context*, for in various ways they direct our attention to contexts or relationships that are important for the study of Stapledon's science fiction novels. Shelton's study of the non-fiction will provide readers of the fiction with insights into Stapledon's philosophical, political, and religious views; Herr moves from a consideration of the fiction on its own terms to suggestive comparisons between Stapledon's unresolved dichotomies and the post-modernist logic of Samuel R. Delany's *The Einstein Intersection*; I examine Stapledon in relation to literary Modernism; Elkins compares Stapledon's cosmic perspective to aspects of Hegelian, Spenglerian, and Marxist thought;

Tremaine draws on anthropological studies for his argument that experience in *Odd John* and *Sirius* is structured by ritual; and Smith's account of the epistolary battles with "Ignotus" places Stapledon squarely within the context of the political debates of the thirties. The final contribution, however, suggested the appropriateness of the present title, for "Letters to the Future" is indeed part of the legacy of Olaf Stapledon. Addressed to an imaginary great-grandson (but dedicated by Robert Crossley to Stapledon's actual great-grandchildren), "Letters" reiterates the faith that a "radical Worldliness" is essential for the spiritual development of the human race. That faith remains one of the most enduring and attractive qualities of Stapledon's science fiction, and its expression here provides an appropriate conclusion to this new collection of critical perspectives on Stapledon and his work.

1

The Moral Philosophy of Olaf Stapledon

Robert Shelton

Olaf Stapledon was a man of letters. Although he is far bettern known today for such classic and influential science fiction novels as *Last and First Men* (1930), *Odd John* (1935), *Star Maker* (1937), and *Sirius* (1944), he also wrote nine non-fiction books and hundreds of reviews, lectures, and articles. In these gently didactic, expository texts, Stapledon laid out many of the major themes (e.g., personality, community, waking, spirit, myth) which are expressed more indirectly in the novels. Common to all the works is a fundamentally moral vision, one tempered by detachment and skepticism while being simultaneously drawn to ecstatic joy and revolutionary zeal.

In this essay, I will describe and analyze Stapledon's philosophical, political, and religious ideas about morality, using three representative non-fiction works: *A Modern Theory of Ethics* (1929), *Waking World* (1934), and *Saints and Revolutionaries* (1939). Published at five-year intervals, these texts highlight the evolution of Stapledon's thinking during this most productive decade, 1929–1939.[1] While all his books and articles have significant philosophical, political, and religious facets, in these three non-fiction texts we can see his emphasis move from, first, the philosophical (in *A Modern Theory of Ethics*), to the political (in *Waking World*), and finally to the religious (in *Saints and Revolutionaries*). All three books examine morality from all three perspectives, but, as Stapledon's sense of purpose and audience shifts, so too does his focus. Still, although these changes are significant, more important is Stapledon's persistent and constant search for a meaningful way to connect the individual and society, that is, for a way that could raise that issue above the level of bromide and cliché.

Furthermore, each of these texts illustrates Stapledon's habit of challenging the limitations of established rhetorical forms. Not only was Stapledon reexamining what was meant by such loaded terms as "morality," "philosophy," "politics," and "religion," he was also changing the contours of the orthodox structures which the specialists had deemed suitable for serious discourse in these fields. For instance, *A Modern Theory of Ethics* concludes with cosmological speculations criticized by most of its reviewers as inappropriate for a philosophical treatise.[2] In *Waking World*, Stapledon expresses his disagreements with H. G. Wells' utopian programs by means of an explicitly Wellsian outline of social history, stretching the master's form to make it contain new and alien topics.[3] *Saints and Revolutionaries* was the tenth volume edited by R. Ellis Roberts for the Heinemann series of personal statements called, collectively, *I Believe*; however, Stapledon's book turned out to be an extended credo by someone unable to declare "I believe."

My main purpose in this essay will be to discuss the non-fiction in its own terms rather than, as has usually been the case, strictly in terms of the novels.[4] Unlike Leslie Fiedler, who dismisses all the non-fiction soundly with such comments as "only one of these books, I believe, was ever published in America, and none is now in print anywhere; nor would I wish it otherwise" (149), I am glad to have a chance to read and study Stapledon's philosophical, political, and religious texts. I am not claiming that Stapledon's non-fiction is more important or more interesting than the novels, merely that it helps enrich our understanding of Stapledon's world view. In both modes he is fundamentally a writer of ideas, more comfortable with grand abstractions than with acute particulars. The non-fiction texts are largely essays which examine, among many other topics, his own myths, ones usually created in and for the fiction. His central explanatory myth, as I conclude, is a concept he calls "personality-in-community." With that myth, Stapledon simultaneously explores the mind and the cosmos.

Without the non-fiction we would also not have as full a record of Stapledon's struggles for self-definition. This claim introduces my second purpose: to show how Stapledon's non-fiction, specifically *A Modern Theory of Ethics*, *Waking World*, and *Saints and Revolutionaries*, presents an apologia, an internalized (and perhaps unconcious) debate about "the self-contained unit of experience" named Olaf Stapledon. The main categories of mood, mind, and character that he describes in these three texts—moral zeal, disillusion, and ecstasy in *A Modern Theory of Ethics*; the animal, the human, and the superhuman in *Waking World*; and the saint, the skeptic, and the revolutionary in *Saints and Revolutionaries*—are all discussed by Stapledon in a fashion which exposes the author as much as it expounds a philosophy. The moral philosophy is at once Stapledon's *and* Stapledon. His prose and his life offer a complex answer to that quintessential utopian question, "how then shall we live?"

In the 1920s Stapledon published a series of essays in academic philosophy journals, leading to *A Modern Theory of Ethics* in 1929 but not to the regular university appointment that his graduate studies at Liverpool University (Ph.D., 1925) had prepared him for.[5] Although it was not Stapledon's first book (with his father's financial assistance, he had a slim volume of poems published just before World War I), *A Modern Theory of Ethics* is his first mature work.[6] More importantly, it can be seen in large measure as a source book for understanding the philosophy conveyed by all the works that follow, including Stapledon's science fiction.

Comparing the openings of *A Modern Theory of Ethics* and Wells' *The War of the Worlds* (1898) suggests that Stapledon's non-fiction can also be seen as a kind of intermediate step between Wells' scientific romances and Stapledon's philosophical fiction. In *The War of the Worlds*, the coming of the Martians hastens society's movement from complacency to disillusionment, from the nineteenth into the twentieth century. This movement also figures in the opening sentence of *A Modern Theory of Ethics*: "It is a commonplace that ours is an age of disillusionment, and that we follow on an age of complacency." I am not suggesting that Stapledon had the first page of *War of the Worlds* (on which appear these key terms, "complacency" and "disillusionment") open before him as he wrote the first sentence of *A Modern Theory of Ethics*. Nonetheless, it is a curious coincidence that Wells' scientific romance and Stapledon's philosophical text should both introduce essentially the same transitions in the same language.[7]

More significantly, his first sentence indicates that Stapledon's analysis of the most basic problem in ethics—defining "good" and "bad"—will consider political, historical, cultural, and psychological questions as well. Stapledon maintains that the definitions of good and bad are in serious need of revision (or re-vision) in the twentieth century. Our old confidence in the meanings of good and bad has been eroded on three main fronts, by what Stapledon categorizes as three profound doubts: cosmological, psychological, and ethical. I take these doubts to symbolize, in essence, the modern transformations of man's relationships respectively, with the universe, with himself, and with others of his own kind. These are key categories not only for *A Modern Theory of Ethics* but also for many Stapledon books that follow. Readers familar with his science fiction will immediately see the relevance of the cosmological to such sweeping works as *Last and First Men* and *Star Maker*; what Stapledon means more specifically by "the psychological" and "the ethical" informs those texts as well as, more directly, *Odd John* and *Sirius*, where new forms of intelligence and new standards of social and private behavior are central themes.

Stapledon rightly claims that these three doubts were "creeping into the minds of thoughtful persons even in that distant age which ended in 1914" (*Ethics* 2). For him, these concerns characterize the modern condition. They also suggest that our responses to those doubts must also be multifaceted and modernized. In other words, a truly *modern* theory of ethics, while acknowledging the traditions of, say, Aristotle and Spinoza, would examine "certain modern ethical theories... in relation with other contemporary movements of the mind" (*Ethics* v). Principal among the modern ethical theorists Stapledon is attracted to are the "Emergent Evolutionists," Lloyd Morgan, C. D. Broad, Alfred North Whitehead, and Samuel Alexander.[8] Their ideas of the good are, in effect, placed between the positions of G. E. Moore and G. C. Field, major English philosophers of the generation before Stapledon's. Typically, Stapledon is building a bridge between apparently opposed points of view, to reconcile, as he puts it in his chapter subtitles, the "Ethical Differences of Professor Moore and Professor Field" in an "Ethical Compromise Between These Theories" (*Ethics* vii). That is, as one reviewer of *A Modern Theory of Ethics* observed, "Prof. Field is right in supposing that *teleological activity* is implied in the existence of 'good,' but Prof. Moore is right in denying that *mental activity* or Consciousness is implied, because teleological activity is not essentially mental" (Lamont 383–84).

Let me translate the philosophical jargon. Stapledon asserts that teleological activity is "the all-pervading miracle of the universe" (*Ethics* 228). More simply put, Stapledon's philosophy is founded on the supposition that everything, "from a piece of lead to a symphony," is a mode of purposeful or "designed" activity. One question raised by this, of course, is who or what is responsible for the design. Emergent evolutionary philosopher C. D. Broad gets around that bothersome conundrum through such definitions as "a system, he says, is teleological 'provided it acts *as if* it were designed for a purpose' " (*Ethics* 82; Stapledon's italics). Broad's "as if" can be traced forward to *Star Maker* or sideways, as it were, to Stapledon's effort in *A Modern Theory of Ethics* to find an ethical theory not divorced from metaphysics or, as some would have it, mysticism.

Along with modern ethical theories, *A Modern Theory of Ethics* also examines "contemporary movements of the mind." In fact, Stapledon's subtitle, *A Study of the Relations Between Ethics and Psychology*, tells us early on to consider the role of psychology in the updating of a theory of ethics. But, as Stapledon well knew, more than one school of thought in his time would insist that there is no relationship between ethics and psychology worth investigating philosophically. For example, "In the eyes of the Logical Positivists, moral theory is either simply a branch of psychology, or else it is nonsense."[9] In contrast, Stapledon holds that "ethics has been too sternly isolated as a self-contained science." He continues, "Biology, psychology, and ethics are certainly distinct sciences; yet if we would properly understand the principles of any one of them, we must bear in mind the principles of both the others" (*Ethics* 12).

In Stapledon's theory, the other two sciences give to ethics nothing less than Life—life seen externally through biological processes (tendencies), and internally through psychological processes (conation). Thus enriched, Stapledon's theory of ethics turns those teleological activities mentioned above from mere philosophical abstractions into more fully human activities. The middle third of *A Modern Theory of Ethics* is taken up by Stapledon's (overly) thorough examination of these esoteric issues such as tendency and teleology. But lest these seem like little more than academic exercises, I should assert that Stapledon is working toward nothing less than a new foundation for morality. In these central chapters, he creates a strong argument for detaching obligation from egoistic subjectivity. As another of his reviewers observed, "notions of obligations cannot be effective when there is nothing to obligate us" (Smith 848).

What, therefore, can be the source of morality? Stapledon's answer to this question returns us to his opening three doubts about man's relationships with the universe, with himself, and with others of his own kind. It also leads us to the more speculative sections of *A Modern Theory of Ethics*. In its tenth chapter, "Objective Activity as the Ground of Ethics," Stapledon works out what is for him a logical basis for obligation: "The good is objective and universal. It does not depend on any particular individual's pleasure, nor on his conation" (*Ethics* 181). The universe is not really an abstraction for Olaf Stapledon; often it is a concrete character in his fiction and the corner-stone of his ethical theory. Stapledon feels that we are obliged to meet the needs of the universe even if it has no needs. Readers of *Star Maker* will recognize the dynamics of that paradox in the following passage from *A Modern Theory of Ethics*:

> *If* the universe as a temporal organic whole has or could have needs, we are morally bound by it. If not, we are still bound by the sum of needs within it, simply for their own sake. If, on the other hand, the universe is a supra-temporal organic whole, and necessarily perfect, then indeed, moral obligation is not relevant to it. But in my last three chapters I shall try to show that we may and do have ethical experience in relation to it, namely, we may admire it for the perfection of its fulfillment. (*Ethics* 182–83)

In addition to the foreshadowing of *Star Maker*, this Idealist's contention (regarding the literal universality of goodness as the ground of moral obligation) provides an important link between Stapledon's philosophical and political visions in *A Modern Theory of Ethics*. That is, those same "tendencies" which led Stapledon to connect the biological and the teleological also now lead him to connect the psychic and the social. Specifically, Stapledon classifies the "tendencies which entail the inter-relation of organisms" under three headings: (1) those essential to the nature of all organisms, e.g., food;

(2) those "only reducible to the innate *social* nature of individual organisms, e.g., sexual behavior"; and (3) those which "emerge from the *psychical* relation of the individual to his own social environment" (*Ethics* 126–128; Stapledon's italics). Under this third tendency Stapledon includes politics, science, art, philosophy, and religion—which are the topics he explores at length in his next book of non-fiction, *Waking World*.

In *A Modern Theory of Ethics*, however, these concerns are basically conflated as the psychic acts of high tendencies. Perhaps in a rush toward his cosmological conclusion, Stapledon makes such assertions about society as "society, in fact, is not only a means to fuller knowledge of the real, and more just conation of its ends; it is also itself an emergence of the real into richer being" (*Ethics* 222). Although Stapledon begins this text with solidly grounded political and historical justifications for modernizing ethics, his conclusion leads him, I believe, from the philosophical to a realm where the cosmological and the religious overlap. And, significantly, he reaches that realm via personal, psychological experience.

The most original material in *A Modern Theory of Ethics* comes in its last two chapters, "Moral Zeal, Disillusion, and Ecstasy" and "Ecstasy and Ethical Theory." In the previous thirteen chapters Stapledon kept his Idealist inclinations in check. In these last two chapters, as he directly acknowledges, he loosens that self-imposed restraint:

> The following argument, of course, owes very much to the absolutism of the great Idealists. While such matter is wholly unreliable (so it seems to me), as the foundation of a philosophical system, it is not out of place in this frankly extravagant speculation. (*Ethics* 266)

These closing chapters of *A Modern Theory of Ethics* suggest that Stapledon, in his non-fiction as well as his fiction, may well be at his best when extravagant.

Moral zeal, disillusion, and ecstasy are "three moods which the mind may experience with regard to good and evil" (*Ethics* 241). These are rare moods since daily reality transpires at levels far below those required to shock (moral zeal), stun (disillusion), or sweep (ecstasy) people into these states. In other words, we don't often feel life as a whole, which, Stapledon says, is required in order to know good and evil. More particularly, moral zeal "consists in a white-hot indignation against all that is conceived as bad" (*Ethics* 242). This mood is not simply anger, for it has a strongly ethical dimension that compels one to change the world.[10] From this state we may fall into the next, disillusion, which is "experienced as a definite contraction of the spirit, or a collapse from a more alive to a less alive mode of being" (*Ethics* 243). In this state we are unable to care about the differences between good and evil. Stapledon's concern here is with a radical contraction or collapse of spirit, one that would all but completely demoralize an entire people and leave them close to existential ennui. As I argue elsewhere, this mood is too much the special province of the twentieth century; it is also central to the message of Stapledon's *Last and First Men*.[11]

Ecstasy takes Stapledon much longer to describe, and so it should, for it is far more important to the overall argument of *A Modern Theory of Ethics* than are moral zeal or disillusion. Similar to aesthetic, religious, and mystical experiences, the ecstatic, however, need not involve art, God, or mystical introspection, although those varieties of ecstatic experience do occur. Two aspects distinguish Stapledonian ecstatic moods: "they are all occasions of intense psychical activity, and all occasions of defeat" (*Ethics* 248). This psychic activity is not "super-normal"; "it is not insight into the 'reality' behind 'appearances,' but discovery of a hitherto unappreciated excellence of the familiar world itself" (*Ethics* 246).[12] It is not dependent, finally, on there being anything behind appearances. "What we see is what we saw before, but we see it solid" (*Ethics* 247). Rather, the intensity of the ecstatic mood comes from the exaltation of the wholeness of the universe —Emergent Evolutionist theory taken to its limit.

By this late point in *A Modern Theory of Ethics* few readers would be at all surprised by the first distinguishing characteristic of the ecstatic mood: it should be associated with "intense psychical activity." However, the second distinguishing characteristic of the ecstatic mood might come as a surprise, at least until we have historicized and personalized this ultimate mood. Stapledon's ecstatic mood, in this light, can be seen as a modernization of tragic catharsis, or, more accurately, of that moment in real life which is akin to the instant when catharsis begins. The following paragraph evokes the horrors of war and, in particular, Stapledon's most intense moments as an ambulance driver in World War I:

> It is possible, for instance, to be on the verge of panic, to be reduced to quivering incapacity and terror, and yet all the while to be an exultant onlooker, rapt in observation of the spectacle, yet in a queer way aloof. It is possible even in the compulsive reaction to pain in one's own flesh, and even while helplessly watching a beloved's pain, to be, precisely, in the very act of frantic revulsion, coldly, brilliantly, enlightened, not as to the excellence of pain, but as to the excellence of the universe. (*Ethics* 248)

Compare these claims to Stapledon's account of his "Experiences in the Friends' Ambulance Unit" (372): "One seemed even to catch surprising glimpses of a kind of super-human beauty in the hideous disaster of war itself." The parallels, in sound and sense, help support my secondary thesis, namely, that *A Modern Theory of Ethics* conveys, along with a rather abstract and esoteric philosophical argument, an effort on Stapledon's part to understand his own experiences. If anything, the philosopher's mask made Stapledon freer to explore the ramifications of his terror; his brief autobiographical account of the war is typically more modest and unassuming.

Within the scope of the argument of *A Modern Theory of Ethics*, the ecstatic mood serves to link ethics, psychology, and cosmology. On those occasions of intense psychic activity the ecstatic person sees a new basis for defining good and bad. That is, "though from our high out-look we can now regard all familiar values with complete detachment, we at the same time see them to be irradiated by the supreme excellence" of the universe itself (*Ethics* 253). As Laurence Sears (472) concludes, *A Modern Theory of Ethics* presents a " 'contract theory' of morals, only in this case the contract is made with the universe." Understandably, Sears refuses to make the leap with Stapledon from a biological to a hyperbiological plane, from temporality to supratemporality. Consciousness is temporal and psychological, but the highest good, Stapledon suggests, may be eternal and cosmological; therefore, he asks, how are we to bridge the two? By admiring, in the ecstatic state, the ideal of the universe, "we experience a supreme fulfillment" (*Ethics* 270). This last point returns us to teleology and emergence—and, significantly, politics:

> At an earlier stage we said that the ideal was that the whole universe should achieve organism, and progressively fulfil its capacity upon the highest of all emergent levels. All our human endeavour, we said, however microscopic its scope, must be controlled in relation to that end. And clearly the only way for us as a race to serve in this cosmical task is to strive to organize our tiny planet and facilitate, if may be, the development of even richer, subtler and more unified mind. (*Ethics* 272–73)

Chronologically and thematically, *Waking World* sits in the middle of my argument. It appeared midway through Stapledon's major decade, and its political focus is situated between his emphases on philosophical and religious questions. In *Waking World* Stapledon looks back explicitly at many of the points he raised in *A Modern Theory of Ethics*. For example, *Waking World*'s tenth chapter, "Philosophy," reintroduces us to "the enterprise of *trying* to see things whole" (*WW* 164). Later in the same chapter Stapledon touches briefly on such now familiar topics as the differences between biological and psychological connotations of "instinct" and "the essential meanings of 'good' and 'bad' " (*WW* 166). In *Waking World*'s next chapter, "Religion," Stapledon lays out the key terms and arguments of *Saints and Revolutionaries*, and then at the very end of *Waking World* he pronounces, "at bottom the party of the new world must at all cost be both revolutionary and in a special sense religious" (*WW* 272), thus stating the main theme of the later book.

This is not to say that *Waking World* is not interesting or important by itself. Thanks to the success, not of *A Modern Theory of Ethics* but of *Last and First Men*, Stapledon can now (c. 1934) write to a much larger audience than he had only five years before. Significantly, even though his fiction was more popular, Stapledon did not abandon non-fiction (McCarthy 26). The more direct form of expression continued to be an important component, it seems, in his efforts to modernize ethics. Although he had abandoned the specialized discourse of academic philosophy—and thereby increased his potential audience all the more—he had not stopped seeking a moral basis for public and private behavior.

Changes in his own circumstances, along with the profound political and economic changes in Europe and America between 1929 and 1934, all contribute to a simplification of Stapledon's style but not of his ideas. His tone in *Waking World* is more consistently colloquial than in *A Modern Theory of Ethics*, with its fairly extreme range of diction.[13] Also, when Stapledon becomes more identifiable as a political writer in the grand socialist-utopian tradition, he is brought more immediately into competition (unwanted on both sides) with H. G. Wells. That is to say, although I agree with Robert Crossley's underplaying of the Wells-Stapledon connection in terms of their science fiction, *Waking World* gives us a direct instance of Stapledon "invading" Wells' territory (Crossley, 1986; 21–24).

In both writers' political non-fiction, the central topics are wisdom, will, and the world state. On the "world-aim" as the social ideal, Stapledon concurs fully with Wells. Stapledon calls for federalization of the planet, more efficient and fair distribution of its resources, and the opportunity for all people to contribute their best to the entire enterprise. In fact, Stapledon's argument in *Waking World* for a global society—a Cosmopolis—sounds so much like Wells' in *The Open Conspiracy: Blueprint for a World Revolution* (1928) that one of Stapledon's critics, C. E. M. Joad, nearly accused him of plagiarism.[14] This was hardly the case, as Stapledon makes emphatically clear in the second section of his introduction, "Another Outline," where, for four pages, Stapledon discusses his agreements and disagreements with "the world's chief outliner" (*WW* 10). After confessing that he has "learnt much from Mr. Wells," Stapledon then separates his point of view from Wells' on philosophical and psychological grounds, not political:

> With diffidence, but also with firmness, I would suggest, then, that the insufficiency of Mr. Wells lies in the superficiality of his view of human nature, and the consequent triviality of his particular kind of humanistic ideal. (*WW* 13; see Shelton 11)

For Stapledon, Wells' brand of humanism is finally too materialistic and yet not materialistic enough. Stapledon sees the Wellsian political perspective as too firmly rooted in biology, and consequently, Wells is, at one end, "not Communist enough in social principles" (*WW* 12), and at the other end, too dismissive of spiritual values. In the categories of Stapledon's next book, Wells is neither revolutionary nor saint. In the central categories of *Waking World*—the animal, the human, and the superhuman—Wells' style of humanism provides a valuable bridge between the first and second categories but, for Stapledon, it ignores the latter, more abstract notion.

While describing his differences with Wells, Stapledon reveals a great deal about his own background and qualifications for writing, as he calls it, this "book of dogmas" (*WW* 7). He deems himself a " 'plain man,' though one who has had the opportunity of wandering from field to field of thought" and who, partly as a by-product of those wanderings, has "a certain imaginative power of 'seeing things whole' " (*WW* 9). These attributes may not at first seem very noteworthy; however, we should recall the discussions on emergence and wholeness in *A Modern Theory of Ethics* and realize that this modest personal claim can also be seen as something of a cosmic gift. On the more mundane level, Stapledon also confesses here to being bourgeois, to living "chiefly on dividends and other ill-gotten gains, even while I proclaim that the system on which I live must go" (*WW* 11). These revelations, like the (partial) founding of the ecstatic mood theory on his own experiences, personalize Stapledon's philosophical and political visions. They also anchor his moral theories in his own moral dilemmas. He is not simply telling us what to do; he is also showing us what he has done and how he has come to understand actions.

Waking World begins with the problem of wisdom: "the present crisis in the affairs of man can be summed in a sentence. He has gained mechanical power, but he had not gained wisdom" (*WW* 1). The trouble, Stapledon continues, is "that there is something more seriously wrong with the world even than economic and social disorder," not that those disorders are not urgent. Their effects are felt throughout Stapledon's outline, from his descriptions of unemployment and the mechanization of industry to his critiques of communism and fascism. Each of these concerns, were Stapledon to analyze and defend them thoroughly, would fill a book if not a career. The structure of *Waking World*—its fifteen brief chapters covering a daunting variety of disciplines—suggests that no single discipline or perspective offers itself as a cure for the lack of wisdom.

What, then, is to be done? Because Stapledon's focus changes so often in *Waking World*, that question raises several different but related answers. The first and next-to-last answer is the Wellsian world state. "This is the kind of world we desire when we think seriously of the world as a whole" (*WW* 21). Then, near the end of *Waking World*, Stapledon returns to this utopian ideal, but he does so with a small yet revealing twist: his penultimate chapter is entitled "World-Revolution?" It is a small thing, but that question mark truly does typify Stapledon's style of thinking. As he will claim in *Saints and Revolutionaries*, Stapledon is a skeptic even about those ideas he most passionately supports.

He is also something of the balanced skeptic when it comes to the second component in the problem of wisdom, namely, the role of modern science. His point of view, he claims, is "at once very friendly toward modern science and very critical" (*WW* 7). Stapledon's concern is, simply put, that modern science and technology will be "prostituted," put to use for the exploitation and not the awakening of humanity. Like Reinhold Niebuhr, Stapledon is repulsed by the base materialism and commercialism of present-day science and technology but he is also stimulated by the notion that, with the right change in attitude, science could make a global community feasible.[15] In a word, science must become a "spiritualizing" influence (*WW* 109).

At present, Stapledon asserts that science is harmful not only because "we use its inventions to destroy one another or enslave one another, but also because it may confuse our minds" by expounding a theory of mechanism over the principle of teleology (*WW* 111). The theory of mechanism Stapledon derives from physics; the teleology principle, as readers of *A Modern Theory of Ethics* will recall, he derives from philosophy and religion.[16] As always, Stapledon places greater emphasis on the workings of ideas than on the workings of things—quite literally, it is a case of mind over matter.

Wisdom also suggests *Waking World*'s "main theme, namely an account of man as a strange medley of three natures, the animal, the distinctly human, and a halting and bewildered propensity toward the superhuman" (*WW* 15). Stapledon devotes a full chapter, the fourth, to "Animal and Man," in which he argues that man is an animal and is more than an animal. More significantly, he devotes, in a largely indirect fashion, this entire book to that third nature, the superhuman. Without the movement toward and past consciousness, Stapledon's book would be more narrowly political. But with the crucial addition, *Waking World* melds the philosophical and the religious with the political. This melding is reflected initially in its title, for "waking" is indeed one of Stapledon's special words. In the Glossary to *Star Maker* he defines "waking": "I have used this word as practically equivalent to 'mental developing.' This seems to have three aspects, knowing, feeling, and willing; or in technical language, cognition, affection, and conation" (*SM* 270). In *Waking World*, Stapledon defines the ruling motive of the world community in almost the same language: "the aim of developing human capacity toward true and comprehensive knowing, discriminate feeling, and appropriate willing" (*WW* 152). Revealingly, in both definitions Stapledon places knowing before feeling, thereby altering the *pathema-mathema-poeima* (feel, know, make) cycle of Greek philosophy.

And finally, as these definitions of "awake" confirm, everything rests on the will. Stapledon makes this point quite clear when he entitles his last chapter "The Will for Change." Appeals for a world order, based even partly on the strength (or triumph) of the will, are dangerous things indeed, and I am not sure that Stapledon fully overcomes those dangers in *Waking World*. There are dark corners in his philosophy. In fact, Stapledon's very first publication, "The Splendid Race" (1908), "discusses the use of eugenics to fashion an improved race" (Satty and Smith 97). Twenty-six years later Stapledon writes, "By every means discoverable, by changes political, economic, educational, and some day eugenical, we must change human nature" (*WW* 163).

In contrast, Stapledon's idea in *Waking World* about swapping the military and educational budgets strikes a lighter note, one that epitomizes Stapledon's utopian political passion and reminds us that he was a teacher:

> The vast sums now spent on armaments might all be transferred to education. The sanity of a community may be roughly measured by the proportion of its income which it assigns to genuine education. By genuine education I mean not merely vocational training, but education for the development of personality. (*WW* 261)

For an Aldous Huxley, such mixtures of utopian optimism and yearnings for totalitarian biological controls would be grist for dark and troubling satire.

In the closing sentence of *Olaf Stapledon: A Man Divided*, Fiedler opines,

> As [Stapledon's] bipolar titles have all along declared, *Last and First Men*, *Darkness and the Light*, *Saints and Revolutionaries*, *Philosophy and Living*, *A Story Between Jest and Earnest*, *A Fantasy of Love and Discord*, Stapledon was a man divided, in whose imagination thesis and antithesis aspired toward a synthesis they could never attain (222).

Fiedler's remark is wonderfully insightful—and wonderfully wrong. It reveals that he is expecting synthesis and, more tellingly, faulting Stapledon's imagination for somehow not achieving it. In contrast, I believe that Stapledon devoted his life to avoiding simple syntheses. Instead of Fiedler's thesis/antithesis/synthesis paradigm, Stapledon's writings present a modernization of the Hegelian dialectical process whereby "antithesis" becomes "complement" (a term favored by Wells) so that "synthesis" can become "symbiosis" (a term borrowed from biology by Stapledon himself). In *Saints and Revolutionaries*, Stapledon applies this thesis/complement/symbiosis pattern—calling it a "twofold dialectic"—to three temperaments, the saint, the skeptic, and the revolutionary (*SR* 22). Ultimately, that process is one of cooperation rather than fusion.

Like *A Modern Theory of Ethics* and *Waking World*, *Saints and Revolutionaries* ends with "Mainly Speculations" and begins in "To-day." In the later book, those are the actual titles of Stapledon's chapters as well as descriptions of their contents. In all three texts, Stapledon begins with a statement of purpose which locates his argument in the politics of the day. The ideologies of fascism and communism, for example, preface all three texts, be their central concerns ethics, the world state, or love and reason. Likewise, Stapledon ends all three texts with considerations of "the cosmical process" (*SR* 160). Structurally, *Saints and Revolutionaries* differs from the other two books, however, in that its middle chapters are more important, more interesting, and more revealing.

While it is clearly true that *Saints and Revolutionaries* has, as Fiedler noted, a bipolar title, its argument actually comes in three more or less equal parts, chapters two, three, and four. In each chapter Stapledon analyzes a type of personality (saint, skeptic, and revolutionary) by relating it to one of the major ideas which dominate his moral philosophy and life. This pattern is explicitly a twofold dialectical process, moving from "Saints, and Pacifism" to "Skeptics, and Morality" to "Revolutionaries, and Metaphysics." Each chapter highlights a facet of Stapledon's vision: the religious, the philosophical, and the political. *Saints and Revolutionaries* as a whole brings the facets together, demonstrating indirectly the folly in compartmentalizing Stapledon's vision. On the other hand, not making distinctions between his different emphases—carping, as Fiedler does, about Stapledon merely repeating himself over and over—would also be wrong.[17] Philosophically and biologically, does not repetition with difference define evolution?

True saints are exceptional people, and "though some of them are consciously religious, others are not" (*SR* 25). Furthermore, Stapledon sees many potential saints among people "who for one reason or another have been violently repelled by the insincerity of conventional religion" (*SR* 25). His saints fit no simple, traditional profile, a point which greatly aids Stapledon in his overall polemical purpose—to raise a pool of awakened citizens of the world, some drawn from the heroic ranks of saints, others from the complementarily heroic revolutionary camps, and still others from the unheroic skeptics. Saints differ from the angelic, those who never "had to pass through the saint's agony of heart-searching and self-discipline" (*SR* 34). The true saint's gentleness and strength are the products of introspection. Although it is not easy to do, one can learn—in and for the real world—to become more saintly. For that project, Stapledon's *Philosophy and Living* (1939) might be a helpful guideline.

Why are saints needed? To reform the world, Stapledon contends, through their "constant attempt to behave with friendliness toward all men" (*SR* 26), especially when they can deal with them directly and individually. This friendliness is one form of the third "tendency" of organisms to interrelate, as described in *A Modern Theory of Ethics*. Saints are inspired to often heroic actions by their generous feelings for their fellow humans—feelings which "emerge from the *psychical* relation of the individual to his own social environment" (*Ethics* 128; Stapledon's italics). More particularly, these feelings render saints "strongly inclined toward pacifism" (*SR* 37). Their psychic relation is nearly empathic; feeling what others feel is literally their passion.

Like saints, revolutionaries often experience moral zeal, and they too are inspired by generous feelings for their fellow human beings: "the genuine revolutionary and the genuine saint habitually and heroically transcend the urge of self-regard" (*SR* 93). The differences between the saint and the revolutionary, however, are crucial. Those differences drive the dialectic of *Saints and Revolutionaries* toward not a synthesis but a symbiosis. First, the thesis (saint) and complement (revolutionary):

> But between the genuine saint and the genuine revolutionary there is a great gulf, which appears not only in their professions but in their behaviour. The saint is chiefly concerned with individuals and their personal relations with one another. The revolutionary is interested in groups and their mutual repercussions. (*SR* 93)

On one side, the individual might be transformed; on the other, the society. To close this gap, Stapledon calls upon an unlikely, unheroic sort, the skeptic, and an even more unlikely process, the mixing of saint, revolutionary, and skeptic—of the religious, political, and psychological—into a symbiotic moral vision. As befits his mode of thinking, Stapledon wishes in a desperate era for a blending of the disparate.

> To-day the need for revolution and the need for better personal relationships are complementary, and must be pursued together. To-day we cannot be saved by saints alone, nor by revolutionaries alone. Saints and revolutionaries must co-operate. Also they must acquire something of one another's nature. Saints must to some extent become revolutionaries, and revolutionaries saints. (*SR* 99–100)

In retrospect, we can indulge Stapledon his use of "saved" in the above: while *Saints and Revolutionaries* was being printed, Hitler invaded Poland, thereby supporting all too well Stapledon's change of thinking between 1934 and 1939 regarding pacifism and the Nazis. In *Waking World* he says, of the makers of the new world he is proposing, "they will preach militant pacifism, the pacifism which not merely will not take up arms, but condemns and ridicules those who do" (*WW* 248). In *Saints and Revolutionaries* he says, "for my part I am with bitter regret convinced that absolute pacifism springs from an obsession with one good principle at the expense of all others" (*SR* 38–39).

This change partly confirms Stapledon's self-definition offered in the middle of *Saints and Revolutionaries*: "I am by nature specially sympathetic toward scepticism" (*SR* 60–61). Skeptics, in Stapledon's description, are controlled by loyalty to intellectual integrity, and therefore they feel "justified in pointing out that most metaphysical and theological theories are either meaningless or extremely doubtful" (*SR* 71). Skeptics embody the first of the three attitudes—surmise, belief, and conviction—described by Stapledon on the opening page of *Saints and Revolutionaries*: "In 'surmise' I feel a minimum of belief, but not no belief at all."[18] While the philosophical facet of Stapledon is attracted to the skeptics, he divorces his full self from their denial of morality. The skeptic explains "moral feelings in terms of ordinary psychology and sociology" (*SR* 71), a practice Stapledon must find inadequate if he is to help awaken the world from its ethical skepticism.

Although Stapledon comes closest to identifying himself with the skeptics, he is also clearly attracted to the more heroic and active figures of the saint and the revolutionary. They offer two competing theories of morality necessary for Stapledon to complete his moral vision. "Though theoretically Marxists reject all universal ethical principles, in practice they exhort us to sacrifice ourselves in a cause which is at bottom the cause of justice and righteousness" (*SR* 105). The revolutionaries (usually but not always equated with Marxists in *Saints and Revolutionaries*) address those urgent social and economic problems Stapledon outlined in *Waking World*. The saints come closer to addressing the ecstatic wisdom of *A Modern Theory of Ethics*.

In his excellent 1947 overview of Stapledon's philosophy, E. W. Martin reads the twofold dialectical process of *Saints and Revolutionaries* somewhat differently. Martin (212) contends that "Stapledon is himself, intellectually a sceptic, with a bias in favour of the revolutionary. Such a bias is shown in several ways, but perhaps most clearly in the manner in which the claims of religious visionaries are ignored."[19] Unfortunately, Martin does not say who ignores the claims or what the claims are, although we can infer from the rest of his discussion that "visionaries" is the problematic word. If so, then he has missed Stapledon's important contention about his variety of saints, namely, that they are "always at once practical and contemplative" (*SR* 28). Also noteworthy is Stapledon's confession that he too has experienced such visions: "but for my part, when I remember the anti–religious people and their glib arguments, I realize that these obscure phrases of the saints do refer, however misleadingly, to something which I myself in a halting way have known" (*SR* 55–56).

I have been arguing that *Saints and Revolutionaries* reveals the skeptic, the revolutionary, and the saint in Olaf Stapledon. As he announces in its introduction:

> In this book I shall say what it is that I personally have learned from saints, sceptics and revolutionaries. I shall not attempt an historical study of the three movements of feeling and thought. I shall merely trace the twofold dialectical movement of my own mind in this respect. (*SR* 24)

That movement culminates in Stapledon's most important concept, "personality-in-community." The word itself is coined in the last pages of *Saints and Revolutionaries*, but the cluster of ideas suggested by it (and its punctuation) was forming at least since *A Modern Theory of Ethics*.[20]

"Personality-in-community" works to draw together the saintly and the revolutionary modes of love and reason. As suggested by its first direct usage, in "Mainly Speculation," personality-in-community will be the moral lesson to be drawn from the ideal education of tomorrow.

> Education, we must suppose, will be a very different thing from what it now is, for it will be single-mindedly directed toward the creation of responsible world-citizens and the development of such creative powers as each individual possesses. The constant aim will be to increase by every possible means, generation by generation, the capacity of our species for personality-in-community. Men will thus become increasingly diverse and individual, and yet at the same time the race as a whole will become more and more unified in respect of mutual knowledge and of fundamental aims. (*SR* 152–53)

Likewise in *Waking World*, Stapledon associates personality-in-community (without using the term) with education: "all education should have a twofold aim, namely to fit the individual for his work in the world, and to make the most of him as a personality" (*WW* 262). Stapledon's conception of education brings together our two largest spheres, the world and the mind, everyone and ourselves.

What holds this conception together? Whether it is expressed as "personality-in-community" or "individual-in-community" or, to go all the way back to *A Modern Theory of Ethics*, "individuals-in-relation" (*Ethics* 169)—in each case, Stapledon seems to be trying to get language to be instantaneous rather than sequential. Hence his use of the "hyphen IN hyphen" device in these symbiotic coinages.[21] "Personality-in-community" is Stapledon's central myth, for it makes it possible for him to bring together all the facets of his message.[22] We can see, sketchily, the relation of psychology and philosophy in "personality"; in "community" we can see traces of the tensions between the political and the religious; and in the hyphen IN hyphen Stapledon's modernization of the dialectical process.

And finally what we can see in personality-in-community is an answer to that quintessential utopian question, "how, then, shall we live?" As individual personalities in community *and* diverse communities of personalities. Thus Stapledon challenges Hegel's view of "the individual as something less real than society, because less self-complete" (*SR* 124). In *A Modern Theory of Ethics*, couched in the language of emergent evolutionary philosophy, he expresses his moral vision:

> The needs of society are the needs of its individual members, but they are the needs of the individuals-in-relation. And from this relation the distinctly social need emerges. The ideally social individual needs harmonious fulfillment of himself as a private person. (*Ethics* 169)

Even a skeptic might wish for this.

NOTES

1. See Satty and Smith, 2–37, for a full record of Stapledon's production in that decade.

2. Burns, 134: "Having followed him so far, it becomes more than doubtful whether one can speak, as he does, of an ideal for the whole or the cosmos. Is not this carrying the category of 'good' into regions to which it does not belong?"

3. Again the contemporary critics were not pleased. See Joad, 10.

4. Half of the articles on Stapledon in the special 1982 issue of *Science-Fiction Studies* make excellent albeit limited use of his non-fiction. See the Branham, Rutledge, Crossley, and Casillo pieces in that collection.

5. Stapledon had taught in the Worker's Educational Association (W.E.A.) since 1912. As Crossley observes in "Olaf Stapledon and the Idea of Science Fiction," 39, "Stapledon was a teacher long before he became a novelist, and he remained a teacher after his fiction declined in popularity in the late 1940s." His lectures for the W.E.A.

were on history, literature, psychology, and philosophy—the subjects he had studied first at Oxford and then at Liverpool.

6. For a fuller account of *Latter-Day Psalms* and their foreshadowings of Stapledon's science fiction, see McCarthy, 18–21.

7. For more complete discussions of Stapledon's Wellsian connections see Crossley, "Famous Mythical Beasts: Olaf Stapledon and H. G. Wells," and Shelton.

8. Kinnaird, 18–19, discusses the Emergent Evolutionists' conception of "wholeness," tracing it back to Spinoza, as does Stapledon in *Waking World*. Samuel Alexander, by the way, coined the term "space-time," a physical and philosophical concept Stapledon often explores.

9. Sayre-McCord, 84. The Logical Positivists, also known as scientific empiricists and the Vienna Circle, were at the height of their considerable influence on the world of academic philosophy in the 1920s and 1930s.

10. The mood of moral zeal, Stapledon says, may be triggered by "the spectacle of animal suffering" (*Ethics* 242). I found his analysis of that example more than mildly prophetic of the extreme branch of today's animal liberation movement.

11. For a fuller discussion of these moods and their application to Stapledon's first novel, *Last and First Men*, see Shelton.

12. Leslie Fiedler, 49, objects strongly to Stapledon's insistence about "the normalcy and almost universal accessibility of this kind of *ekstasis*."

13. For example, contrast the following sentences from *A Modern Theory of Ethics*: "Then came the war. It gave us something large to do and vivid to think" (*Ethics* 4); "In an earlier chapter we identified fulfillment of tendency with realization of capacity, actualization of potentiality, the bringing into being of a new actuality" (*Ethics* 265). The latter is a style Stapledon (mercifully) gave up after 1929.

14. Joad, 10: "Surely, one feels, one has read something of the kind before. And so one has in Wells' *The Open Conspiracy* and *The World of William Clissold*."

15. Martin, 209, discusses this Stapledon-Neibuhr connection eloquently.

16. "All the laws of physics are based upon inductive observation. There is no demonstrable *necessity* in virtue of which an unsupported stone *must* fall" (*WW* 123).

17. Philmus, 76, reaches this conclusion in reviewing Fiedler, Kinnaird, and McCarthy.

18. "In 'belief,' though I have not certainty, I am ready to bet heavily on the truth of the proposition.... In 'conviction' I have no doubt whatever that the proposition is true. I cannot conceive its being false" (*SR* 1–2).

19. Also, Crossley, in "Politics and the Artist: The Aesthetic of *Darkness and the Light*," 294, contends that Stapledon's "political and educational work expressed that side of himself which was a 'revolutionary' while his visionary writing belonged to Stapledon the 'saint.' " This division, I believe, is too neat, especially if we take into account the ecstatic mood of *A Modern Theory of Ethics*.

20. Kinnaird, 26, is correct, I believe, in saying that the concept of personality-in-community "is first given this phrasing in 1939."

21. In the index to *Olaf Stapledon*, McCarthy, 164, equates "personality-in-community" and "symbiosis" as themes.

22. Kinnaird, 34, describes personality-in-community in terms of a fable which is worth quoting in full:

> A hero, Personality-in-Community, assisted by a forgotten old wizard, Mysticism, is trying to rescue his beloved Spirit from three evil enchanters who are holding her captive—Capitalism,

Materialism, and Ethical Scepticism. The hero's task is to "awaken," by destroying the spell of the enchanters, the Sleeping Beauty of Spirit, then to wed her in true Worship (the union of Saint and Revolutionary), and finally to restore Man and Spirit, thus reunited, to the throne of their ancestors in the Holy City at the World's End, the Community of the World-Revolution.

WORKS CITED

Burns, C. D. Review of *A Modern Theory of Ethics. International Journal of Ethics* 40 (October 1929): 134.

Crossley, Robert. "Famous Mythical Beasts: Olaf Stapledon and H. G. Wells." *Georgia Review* 36 (Fall 1982): 619–35.

———. "Politics and the Artist: The Aesthetic of *Darkness and the Light*." *Science-Fiction Studies* 14 (November 1984): 294–305.

———. "Olaf Stapledon and the Idea of Science Fiction." *Modern Fiction Studies* 32 (Spring 1986): 21–42.

Fiedler, Leslie A. *Olaf Stapledon: A Man Divided*. New York: Oxford University Press, 1983.

Joad, C. E. M. "The New World Order." *The Spectator* (23 November 1934): 10.

Kinnaird, John. *Olaf Stapledon*. [Starmont Reader's Guide, 21] Mercer Island, Wash.: Starmont House, 1986.

Lamont, W. D. Review of *A Modern Theory of Ethics. Mind* 38 (July 1929): 383–84.

Martin, E. W. "Between the Devil and the Deep Sea: The Philosophy of Olaf Stapledon." In *The Pleasure Ground: A Miscellany of English Writing*, ed. Malcolm Elwin. London: MacDonald & Co., 1947.

McCarthy, Patrick A. *Olaf Stapledon*. Boston: Twayne Publishers, 1982.

Philmus, Robert. "Undertaking Stapledon." *Science-Fiction Studies* 14 (March 1984): 71–77.

Satty, Harvey J., and Curtis C. Smith. *Olaf Stapledon: A Bibliography*. Westport, Conn.: Greenwood Press, 1984.

Sayre-McCord, Geoffrey. "Logical Positivism and the Demise of 'Moral Science.' " In *The Heritage of Logical Positivism*, ed. Nicholas Resher. Lanham, Md: University Press of America, 1985.

Sears, Laurence. Review of *A Modern Theory of Ethics. Journal of Philosophy* 26 (15 August 1929): 470–73.

Shelton, Robert. "The Mars-Begotten Men of Olaf Stapledon and H. G. Wells." *Science-Fiction Studies* 11 (March 1984): 1–14.

Smith, T. V. Review of *A Modern Theory of Ethics. The American Journal of Sociology* 35 (1930): 848.

Stapledon, Olaf. "Experiences in the Friends' Ambulance Unit." In *We Did Not Fight: 1914–1918 Experiences of War Resisters*, ed. Julian Bell. London: Cobden-Sanderson, 1935.

———. "Glossary." In *Star Maker*. Los Angeles: Jeremy P. Tarcher, 1987.

2

Convention and Spirit in Olaf Stapledon's Fiction

Cheryl Herr

Between 1945 and his death in 1950, Olaf Stapledon wrote a short story, not published until its appearance in the July 1979 issue of *The Magazine of Fantasy and Science Fiction*, called "A Modern Magician." In this Hawthorn-esque moral fable, a young man named Jim willfully develops psychokinetic powers in overcompensation for unempathic parenting, physical weakness, and lack of confidence. To impress a potential girlfriend, Jim learns to kill small animals, to short-circuit engines, and to perform other tricks by force of will alone. Predictably, his jealousies lead him to murder his girlfriend's brother and ultimately, in a fit of remorse, to commit suicide psychokinetically. Jim's self-implosion might be seen as a Gordian-knot nexus for many of Stapledon's radically interwoven concerns—the nature of selfhood, the role of ethics in the modern world, the relationship between community (or what Stapledon in the story calls "team spirit") and misuses of power, and the mixture of good and evil in the world that makes infinitely problematic anything like self-knowledge, especially when that knowledge is to be achieved on the cosmic as well as the personal level.

What I find interesting about this minor story is how fully it expresses, despite its brevity, a key element in Stapledon's vision; here is a satire that does not cast blame but urges us just to accept the experience and emotions of its characters, to reflect on the paradoxes posed by their fates. Certainly, they are confused human beings. Jim cavalierly disbelieves in the morality that causes him to kill himself. His girlfriend perceives him as compelling precisely because of his surprising blend of infantilism and perversity. Such paradoxical satire finds expression in a style of quiet understatement. Throughout Stapledon's fictions, an attitude of infatuation with fate and of withheld judgement holds sway; unlike many writers of science fiction, Stapledon rarely allows us to hope for a happy ending, but he also never allows us to feel much sorrow that the narrative outcomes sometimes look like disasters.[1] It is symptomatic of his largest aims that one of his favorite adjectives for characters is "odd"; these odd figures walk the borderland between human needs for acceptance and their own social nonconformity, between sanity according to the standards of their culture and an intimation of the universal processes in which they are caught up.

Stapledon sometimes states his themes a good deal more abstractly, of course, than his suggestions of them in "A Modern Magician." For instance, in his small volume *Beyond the "Isms"* (1942), he observes that civilization needs to find "some clear principle . . . for purging all the 'isms' and synthesizing whatever is valuable in them for our guidance. Materialism and spiritism, individualism, and collectivism, are the two dimensions for the shaping of that principle" (*Isms* 6). In general, that book points toward a "double synthesis" of these dichotomies, a synthesis that will take the concept of "spirit" as the guiding principle of right actions (*Isms* 115).[2] According to this logic, what Jim needed was not to eliminate his negative characteristics but to find a better balance between these personality flaws and his considerable intellectual powers; he needed *spirit* to inform his endeavors and those of his world. But Jim could not achieve spiritual enlightenment as he did psychokinetic force, by will alone. Rather, he failed in part because his civilization was in a phase of decline, as evidenced by the moral uncertainty that he and his girlfriend shared. To move beyond his plight, we need to look outside the tiny moment that his story opens up for us. Hence, Stapledon seeks the needed "double synthesis" in fictions that transcend by billions of years the temporal setting which in "A Modern Magician" microcosmically displays Stapledon's dichotomous rhetoric.

Throughout his writing, Stapledon maps out the possibilities for such a synthesis, yet again and again he critiques his dream by describing civilizations which either fail to attain the ideal state or, having reached it, find themselves subject to a variety of natural or manmade disasters. Referring to *The Flames*, *Odd John*, *Star Maker*, and *Last and First Men*, I argue that this persistent undermining in his imaginative works of ideas which Stapledon took quite seriously results from his having centered the novels not on the dichotomies of materialism and "spiritism" or of the individual and the community, but on that of the conventional and the spiritual, a dialectic which his fictions are not entirely aware of and in any event cannot resolve. There are several reasons for this narrative irresolution. First, I document Stapledon's concern with language itself, with the conventions and limitations of expression that keep both the author and his characters from making clear the nature of their various states of enlightenment about the ideal balance of self and society. Then I demonstrate that Stapledon's presentation of the self not as autonomous and self-determining but as derived, at least in part, from cultural conventions, precludes the possibility that his characters or civilizations can attain that personal-communal balance that would nurture ultimate spiritual advancement. Third, I discuss briefly the coalescence of these ideas in Stapledon's masterwork, *Star Maker*.

Finally, in order to position his fiction in our own time, I compare the visionary narrative enterprise of *Star Maker* with Samuel Delany's speculative classic, *The Einstein Intersection* (1967—reprinted in 1986 under the title *A Fabulous, Formless Darkness*). One point of this comparison is to foreground Stapledon's fictional meditations on community as a transitional moment in the history of science fiction utopianism. Stapledon's reasoned blocking of the cosmic-consciousness route to enlightened community has produced the "different" and highly autocritical utopianism that a writer like Delany projects. Another way to state this distinction is to observe that Stapledon is a Modernist writer who shares the teleological preoccupations of his era, which were variously construed by fellow Modernists like D. H. Lawrence, E. M. Forster, and Ford Madox Ford. Delany writes out of a science fictional postmodernism that is postapocalyptic; his writing sympathizes more with the techno-assumptions of cyberpunk than with the specific philosophic dichotomies that exercised Stapledon. Yet, like almost every science fiction writer worth his or her salt, Delany displays indebtedness (whether direct or indirect does not matter, so pervasive is Stapledon's influence) to Stapledon's brand of speculative fiction.

This final point—Stapledon's influence on our present—seems to me not often enough accentuated in the writing about Stapledon. Certainly we do well to explore the relationships between Stapledon and his own forerunners such as Dante and Blake, but the persistence with which Stapledon reaches into our own present continues to fascinate both my students and me.[3] It is enormously useful to trace his significant presence in the writings of Asimov, Heinlein, Clarke (McCarthy 141–46), Vonnegut, and others. But Stapledon's impact comes home even more formidably when I ask science fiction classes to write stories explicitly filling out the slim details that Stapledon gives us about a specific culture. In generating characters and narratives from those details, readers reinvent Stapledon's fiction and by doing so achieve many things—an appreciation of the impact of paradoxical assumptions on character and action, a rethinking of Stapledon's world in terms of our own postmodern one, a clarification of the problems posed by utopian designs in *any* world, and an awareness of Stapledon's sheer scope, the magnitude of his imagination.

I

Again and again, Stapledon's narrators and characters find themselves, when confronted with philosophical questions, at a loss for words. Whether they attempt to understand the nature of "spirit" or to define aesthetic form, Stapledon's personae run up against the conceptual limitations imposed by their culture and enshrined in its vocabulary.[4] Naturally enough, the author himself is also confined by those cultural walls.

From the first of his novels, *Last and First Men* (1930), Stapledon exploits the theme of linguistic inadequacy. For example, the narrator tells us, in a tone that indicates his agreement, that the "care-free" Flying Men "were untroubled by the insatiable lust of understanding" but that "they soon formulated a beautifully systematic account of experience."

> They clearly perceived, however, that the perfect sphere of their thought was but a bubble adrift in chaos. Yet it was an elegant bubble. And the system was true, in its own gay and frankly insincere manner, true as significant metaphor, not literally true... Adolescents were encouraged to study the ancient problems of philosophy, for no reason but to convince themselves of the futility of probing beyond the limits of the orthodox system. (*LFM* 8: 196–97)

The implication is strong here that only those who cease to care about articulating absolute answers can free themselves from the anxiety of philosophical uncertainty.

Other Stapledon narrators are similarly aware of verbal limitations. The narrator of *Star Maker* (1937), for example, faced with the enormously difficult task of explaining and describing his cosmic-mystic vision, notes, "though human language and even human thought itself are perhaps in their very nature incapable of metaphysical truth, something I must somehow contrive to express, even if only by metaphor" (*SM* 14:412). And he adds:

> This poor myth, this mere parable, I shall recount, so far as I can remember it in my merely human state. More I cannot do. But even this I cannot properly accomplish. Not once, but many times, I have written down an account of my dream, and then destroyed it, so inadequate was it. With a sense of utter failure I stammeringly report only a few of its more intelligible characters. (*SM* 14:412–13)

Thus the narrator stammers a truth dimly perceived when he was the "cosmical mind," further dimmed when he returns to his role of ordinary Englishman, and finally trivialized by the rendering in human language of human vision and human memory. Persisting in his self-denigration, he calls the vision itself a "dream" and a "myth" (*SM* 14:413).

Even Stapledon's stories of the personal (as opposed to the cosmic) life provide us with evidence that human language cannot meet the challenges that Stapledon's imagination assigns it. For example, the characters described in *The Flames* (1947) are unable to shape in human language their most significant experiences and feelings. In that short novel, in which fire spirits seek the aid of the character Cass in their quest for a source of radioactive power on Earth, the problems of communication become acute. For one thing, the reader tends to accept the conversation of the flame-being as having actually occurred, even though it is presented to us only indirectly by Cass, who tells of his experience in a letter to his friend Thos. Further, Cass tells Thos that the flame's "consciousness," with which Cass was telepathically in touch, functioned more speedily than his own until "some external influence" helped Cass's mind to keep pace with his visitor's thoughts. Such an assertion cannot help but make the reader wonder, as Thos does, about Cass's narrative reliability. To this description, Cass adds the predictable coda: "it is difficult to find words to describe the little flame's consciousness . . . " (*Flames* 16).

The flame, too, shares Cass's concern over the problem of adequate communication. At first, the flame projects emotions and feelings, but later it grapples with Cass's word-bound mentality to tell him about the nature of flame-existence. In the process, the flame questions:

> Does this mean anything to you? If not, remember that I am trying to describe in a fantastically foreign language things that are strictly indescribable, save in our own language. Human languages are all unsuitable, not only because of their alien concepts, but also because the very structure of the language is alien to our ways of experiencing. (*Flames* 35)

Apparently, the flame's own language is adequate to its needs, but we can deduce from this assumption only that the flame values the conventions that shape its own language, not that the flame, if real, is possessed of truths unavailable to humanity. Still, it remains an open question whether there is in the universe a language that, in its perfect conformity with heightened or utopian experience, might be said to enable community rather than simply to thwart adequate communication.

We might expect from Thos, the apparent spokesperson for human sanity, a greater confidence in words than that of Cass and the flame as well as a firmer hold on philosophic certitudes. But Thos's reaction to his friend's story, presented in the epilogue, is incredulous and confused. Thos tells Cass's tale of the solar flames, who were lucky enough not to have become terrestrial beings cut off from the sun-source of their radioactive life. These solar entities were part of a cosmic community which "was entirely devoted to extra-sensory and metaphysical study of the ultimate reality." Thos adds in parentheses, "so Cass affirmed. For my part, I doubt whether there is really any sense in such a statement. I see no reason to suppose that extra-sensory experience can probe to ultimate reality; and as for metaphysical study, it is nothing but a deceptive juggling with words" (*Flames* 77).

The Flames shows that even very close to the end of his life, Stapledon maintained his initial and essential preoccupation with the problem of linguistic adequacy. Clearly, his fiction moves toward this proposition: that the human self and the nonhuman (or alien) self alike are bound by this problem, and that this binding impedes the search for the spirit which, according to Stapledon, informs the cosmos. The search for spirit is undermined by the inability of the seekers to operate nonlinguistically and unconventionally.

II

When we look at the nature of the individual personality in Stapledon's works, we find that he treats the self as he does the languages of his protagonists. Both language and self are seen largely as cultural artifacts that become obstacles to the apprehension of spiritual reality. We are faced, that is, with the paradox of individuals who crave enlightenment but are disabled by the very mode of their existence and interaction.

Near the beginning of *The Flames*, there occurs a prime demonstration of this thematic coalescence. There, referring to Earth-dwellers both of his own kind and of the flame variety, Cass says, "Thos, we're all human, aren't we, all equally persons? Surely persons ought to be able to feel their fundamental kinship whatever their race. Even if they were of different species, if they were bred in different worlds, surely they ought to accept full responsibility for one another simply in virtue of their personality." Yet, claiming that "alien powers" had infested his thought, Cass goes on to "disown" this statement (*Flames* 10). We note again that Stapledon establishes irresolvable ambiguities. Are the flames using Cass as a mouthpiece or not? Are they unfortunate heroes or conniving enemies to humanity? Personhood, even if universally valued, does not guarantee either the possession of truth or truthful communication. Nor does it have the power to make obvious some aspect of being that may be shared by all sentient creatures—or may not.

We are, of course, prepared to be sympathetic, at first, to beings who state:

> We are gifted with extra-sensory powers far greater than yours, and also with a far more thorough detachment from the enthralling individual self. We are capable also of a more penetrating or soaring imaginative insight into the nature of spirit. (*Flames* 31).

The flames' ability to soar so high comes from their telepathic powers and from the ability of the individual flame to become, at times, the racial consciousness. Like the narrator of *Star Maker*, like the supernormals in *Odd John*, like individuals in *Last and First Men*, a flame can transcend its singleness to reach a higher and more comprehensive state of individuality, to become a community-as-individual. Yet this state is radically unstable in that it does not permanently keep the flames in a state of self-transcendence. Like the Last

Men, who can only remember sadly what it was like to be unified, and like the Flying Men, who are less racially coherent when they are grounded, the flames on Earth yearn nostalgically for their lost solar communality. Enemies or not, they are prepared to use human beings to better their condition. And the imagined reader, subject to his or her enthralling selfhood and (if only because the narrative implicitly assigns the reader this role) committed to defending in that selfhood, can never confidently assess the value of the flame's mission or the adequacy of Cass's response.

The impinging of personality on the search for truth is also taken up in *Odd John*. When still only eight years old, John, who has been studying philosophy, tells the narrator that "religious experience (properly defined) is no evidence... that the universe has a purpose, such as the fulfillment of personality" (*OJ* 5:28). Although John seems bent on fulfilling his nature anyway, he does not see his personal growth as critical to the cosmos. And John insists more on his own multiplicity than on the value of his "odd" selfhood. In fact, he is composed of more than one "I," as he explains to the narrator when telling about his murder of a policeman: "the 'I' that had committed that folly was incapable of realizing how foolish it was being. The new 'I,' that had suddenly awakened, realized very clearly..." (*OJ* 5:33). In addition, he can function on two planes at once: the normally human and the extrasensory. John's differences from ordinary mortals are emphasized when he adopts the identity of a "precocious genius" and visits the Bloomsbury Group (*OJ* 10:65). He returns to tell his friend Fido that the intellectuals he met were simply flies buzzing in a "web, a subtle mesh of convention, so subtle in fact that most of them are unaware of it" (*OJ* 10:65). Their entrapment by species and by the experiences available to upper-class *Homo sapiens* in early twentieth-century London, is fully apparent to John. Where his selfhood is multiple, theirs is merely conventional. But at some level his assertion of multiplicity may be taken merely as ratifying the sense in which his own being composes itself from various conventional roles.

When John finally makes his spiritual breakthrough in the wilderness, it occurs on an emotional rather than an intellectual level, and it involves his recognition that, regardless of whether an experience is potentially painful or pleasant, "form" and "unity" are to be delighted in (*OJ* 12:84). Yet John can never define his understanding for the narrator's enlightenment. Instead, he asserts, "to describe the spiritual life, we should have to remake language from the foundations upwards" (*OJ* 12:86); this seems to me an important point—that the very structure of human language in all of its own multiplicity remains merely crippling in relation to the unthinkable otherness of spiritual predications. What characterizes the supernormal, then, is a duality or multiplicity of consciousness combined with the ability to know without the mediation of language. Possessing this ability, not only John but also the narrator of *Star Maker* (as the cosmic mind) find major value in the aesthetic forms they create or identify; such art supposedly embodies meanings that transcend those ideas available in less ordered forms and in ordinary verbal communication.

Although aesthetic form may hold the key to spiritual knowledge, what Stapledon's novels fail to give us is the conviction that the human self either possesses the ability to use this key or exists as an identifiable and discrete entity. In fact, all of the evidence points in the opposite direction, to the extent that Stapledon disallows the possibility of individual human immortality; such a belief is always the sign of confusion in his human communities.

This questioning of the nature of the self comes to a focus in *Last and First Men* in the speech and experience of the Divine Boy of the Patagonians. Speaking of his attempt to rescue himself after he had been buried in snow, the Boy observes, "...I saw myself, and all of us, through the eyes of the umpire."

> It was as though a play-actor were to see the whole play, with his own part in it, through the author's eyes, from the auditorium. Here was I, acting the part of a rather fine man who had come to grief through his own carelessness before his work was done. For me, a character in the play, the situation was hideous; yet for me, the spectator, it had become excellent, within a wider excellence. I saw that it was equally so with all of us, and with all the worlds. (*LFM* 5:83)

Finding that a person may adopt any number of roles, the Boy implies that the role has priority over anything that we can label "the self." He sees the folly of persisting as though one were not only single but singular, not only a role but a person bound to a role. In this understanding, the Boy, like Odd John to some extent, aligns his insights with those of Zen Buddhism—which has its own distrust of language and its own understanding of individuality and its follies. Just as the Last Men are able to enter supposedly self-contained minds existing in the past, just as the narrator of *Star Maker* is able to bond with supposedly holistic intellects on various planets, so the Divine Boy was able to become, merely by seeing and articulating it, a new kind of multiple self, a virtual non-self composed of many roles: umpire, actor, author, character, person, spectator. Emphatically, being a "person" is to the Divine Boy as much a role as is being an actor or the character he is performing.

One might conclude, as Stapledon seems to wish us to conclude, that the Divine Boy's moment of enlightenment describes Stapledon's ideal of human perspective, in which a person may transcend single vision to adopt another viewpoint so comprehensive as to be considered communal. Yet one must admit that for the reader each character in Stapledon, whether multiple, enlightened, or benightedly single-minded, has the same texture, the same degree of authenticity, the same contour of selfhood as any other. This phenomenon seems to me not only a result of Stapledon's debatable skills as a novelist; his narration occurs through the language which at once limits our perception of character and tailors the speaking being to the demands of linguistic and cultural convention. For this reason, even if Stapledon's narrators and characters "truly" reach a state in which the personality is both heightened and transcended, the text can never demonstrate to our satisfaction what this state is like.

To offset this problem, Stapledon—like Odd John—turns repeatedly to the notion of aesthetic form, a value comparable in its lack of definition in his texts to the notion of community or of enlightened individualism. An important example of Stapledon's sense of aesthetic order in the universe occurs in this description of the Flying Men, who regarded their aerial gymnastics, dances, and passions "with detached aesthetic delight" (*LFM* 8:198). Hence, their "social order" was "in essence neither utilitarian, nor humanistic, nor religious, but aesthetic" (*LFM* 8:199). The narrator adds, "every act and every institution were to be justified as contributing to the perfect form of the community. Even social prosperity was conceived as merely the medium in which beauty should be embodied, the beauty, namely, of vivid individual lives harmoniously related" (*LFM* 8:199).

This aesthetics of community, a social order based on constraints of beauty and form, foregrounds both the limitations and the value of Stapledon's vision. The relationship existing among all the Flying Men is beautiful to those who possess the proper codes for understanding it, to those who can be persuaded to adopt their bubble system of thought. But one has to be taught the rules by which order and beauty are perceived. Hence, Fido cannot interpret the music of the supernormals. Similarly, in *The Flames*, when Cass listens to a flame-poem, we are told that he is terribly moved by the experience and that he saw in it "the God of beauty, truth and goodness" (*Flames* 48) but that he does not understand the aesthetics of the piece well enough to explain them to us. Stapledon, however, does not leave Cass's interpretation unchallenged. In fact, the flame pointedly lectures Cass about the follies of finding the mystical in the uncomprehended.

We can at least tentatively conclude that even the appreciation of aesthetic form fails to provide access for Stapledon's characters to the metaphysical truths and values they seek. In constantly working the themes of language, the self, and art—all as possible means to the establishment of enlightened or spirit-conscious community—Stapledon shows us that we do not need a Martian invasion or the cooling of the sun to create our tragedies. The limitations of linguistic systems, our flawed concepts of personality—in sum, our inability to escape the codings and conventions of culture which by their very nature both enable communication and thwart it—work against the achievement of an ideal synthesis of matter and spirit, of individual and community. More important, his preoccupation with these limitations kept Stapledon from writing narratives which ended not in loss or in resignation but in the exultation of discovery and conviction.

III

In his cosmically comprehensive *Star Maker*, Stapledon's use of the themes I have been tracing demonstrates that the controlling dichotomy of this novel is not the individual and the community but convention and spirit, a highly problematic binarism. The narrator begins his story by considering his life in England and in particular lavishes attention on his marriage as an emblem of all community; he calls the union "our delicate balance of dependence and independence, this coolly critical, shrewdly ridiculing, but loving mutual contact . . . a microcosm of true community" (*SM* 1:256). That communal attachment mirrors his subsequent relationship with Bvalltu, the philosophic Other Man whom the narrator mentally inhabits. As Bvalltu and the narrator gather about them the other minds participating in their journey for truth, the narrator continues to struggle to tell us about his self-perception:

> I, the human individual, can only in a most superficial and falsifying way participate in the superhuman experience of the communal 'I' which was supported by the innumerable explorers. This book must needs be a ludicrously false caricature of our actual adventure. But further, though we were and are a multitude drawn from a multitude of spheres, we represent only a tiny fraction of the diversity of the whole cosmos. Thus even the supreme moment of our experience, when it seemed to us that we had penetrated to the very heart of reality, must in fact have given us no more than a few shreds of truth, and these not literal but symbolic.

And he goes on to hope that his account may have "the kind of truth that we sometimes find in myths" (*SM* 5:300).

The critical notion of the mythic recurs in the narrator's discussion of "The Myth of Creation" (Chapter 14). There the narrator partially disengages himself from the narration, saying more than once that his story states itself within his mind. He is not composing the myth and controlling its outcome; rather, the myth is the means by which the vision he seems to witness is conveyed to the reader—all in a very tenuous communication, for, as he states bluntly, "human language and even human thought itself are perhaps in their very nature incapable of metaphysical truth . . . " (*SM* 14:412).

Though we are not surprised to find a human narrator professing an inability to tell us about his vision, we may be surprised to discover that even in his role of cosmic mind the narrator did not understand himself. He agonizes, " . . . when I tried to probe the depths of my own being, I found impenetrable mystery."

> Though my self-consciousness was awakened to a degree thrice removed beyond the self-consciousness of human beings, namely from the simple individual to the world-mind, and from the world-mind to the galactic mind, and thence to the abortively cosmical, yet the depth of my nature was obscure. (*SM* 12:398)

The narrator emphasizes the obscurity of the self—its purpose, its nature—in several ways. For one thing, he insists that the enduring problem even in the idealized communal life is the problem of the self. When he discusses the nature of avian cloud life, he notes that the "constant danger of the bird-clouds was physical and mental disintegration. Consequently the ideal of the coherent self was very prominent in all their cultures" (*SM* 7:330). This brief insight into the making of ideology reflects the trouble experienced by the narrator and Bvalltu when they decide to explore the cosmos together. Sometimes failing to agree over "future plans," they discover in themselves "terrifying mental disorder" (*SM* 4:295). The insane worlds that the cosmic mind later encounters in his travels demonstrate that such disorientation can occur at any stage in the enlargement of the self from mere individual to composite community. Although Stapledon avers that true community enhances the self as well as the whole, the precious personality is often at fault either for rigidly maintaining its independence from other selves or for destabilizing more utopian states of being.

This is not to say that communality itself is illusory. The narrator definitely states that, in the case of his own alliance with the other beings who formed the cosmic mind, their "community was so perfected that the experiences of each were available to all" (*SM* 8:342). But he does not mask the fact that his understanding of this state is as hazy as his comprehension of the Star Maker's ultimate cosmos: "whether, as experients, we remained many or became one, I do not know. But I suspect that the question is one of those which can never be truly answered because in the last analysis it is meaningless" (*SM* 8:343). In addition, the narrator cannot say how this "utopian" state was engineered by the worlds throughout his cosmos that had achieved it, except to note that human nature on those planets had undergone an unpredictable and "miraculous" change (*SM* 8:346).

Even though the narrator remains unable to describe fully such states and changes, we do find in his description of the "ultimate cosmos" the suggestion that some correspondingly ultimate aesthetic canon and spiritual vision have guided the Star Maker's efforts—or at least evolved from his successive periods of creativity. The narrator observes that in all of these creations, "the goal was conceived, in the end, to include community and the lucid and creative mind" (*SM* 15:427). Later, he adds that

> in the mutual joy of the Star Maker and the ultimate cosmos was conceived, most strangely, the absolute spirit itself, in which all times are present and all being is comprised; for the spirit which was the issue of this union confronted my reeling intelligence as being at once the ground and the issue of all temporal and finite things. (*SM* 15:428–29)

To have proceeded so far in understanding the spirit, though hampered by his human language and prestructured thought, might have pleased the narrator; we might, that is, have been gratified to find the constraints of linguistic convention and the attainment of spiritual vision less at odds when the narrator actually confronts the Star Maker. But the presence of substantial suffering in the ultimate cosmos causes him to reject his vision and to retreat to "the little dark cell of ... [his] separate self" (*SM* 15:429). Here the metaphoric nature of his language comes close to collapsing on itself, for if the Star Maker permeates all parts of its creations, how can the narrator even for a moment escape the vision being offered to him? This impasse paradoxically passes when he notes that *as* he "slammed and bolted the door," his "walls were all shattered and crushed by the pressure of irresistible light" (*SM* 15:429).

Finally, the mind of our less-than-perfect cosmos posits both the immanence of the Creator and the fact that "in truth the eternal spirit was ineffable. Nothing whatever could be truly said about it" (*SM* 15:430). This kind of riddling statement has the effect of the old joke about the compulsive liar who couldn't be trusted even in the statement that he was a compulsive liar, but Stapledon is absolutely serious. We come to understand that his narrator has struggled all along to create significance by resolving persistent distinctions which he now claims to be illusory: the Star Maker and his creation, the self and the community, language and truth. None of these terms or dichotomies can be said to rule where all creation is unified in the Star Maker's ineffable "more ... than spirit" (*SM* 15:430). What are we to make, then, of Stapledon's frequent presentation of both language and the self as largely conventional, as resistant to such spiritual unification? One answer is that Stapledon's novels never came to terms with their central but suppressed dialectic of convention and spirit, an avoidance which, at the very least, makes the fictions less celebration of spirit than somber reminders of the limitations of being human.

IV

Stapledon's novels remind us further that they are expressions of cultural Modernism, a set of movements not a little exercised by precisely the effects of conventionality that Stapledon negotiates. The journey-resignation pattern of *Star Maker* might readily be compared with Eliot's patterning of *The Waste Land* or with Joyce's equilibrist ending to *Ulysses*. In both works, the protagonists struggle to sustain themselves both through and because of their society's norms. But other patterns are possible in the world of postmodern science fiction, and Delany's *The Einstein Intersection* demonstrates one of them. In an epigraphic quotation from his *Writer's Journal* for March 1966, Delany comments, "endings to be useful must be inconclusive" (Delany 129). When Lobey, Delany's antihero, takes off toward darkness at the story's end, we are to understand that he rejects the conventions of both country and city life in favor of his own unpredictable inner rhythm. That rhythm of "difference," which the narrative thematizes, is a lot like some of the ultimate concepts that Stapledon labels ineffable, but Delany's concept seems to me to be distinguished by its endless specificity, not its ultimate ineffability.[5] True, Lobey is not sure about the difference that the future holds, but he knows that his own difference expresses itself in his ability to hear the music that other people are thinking. And he knows that Friza's difference was the psychokinetic power that she shares with Stapledon's hero in "A Modern Magician." In Lobey's world, everyone is on the way to becoming a post-modern, postapocalyptic magician, and their special differences are becoming so pronounced that "functionality" (approximation to a pre-apolcalyptic human norm) is an increasingly irrelevant measure of value.

The "different" world that Lobey accedes to pointedly does not build on previous traditions such as stable marriages and respect for elders. Although Lobey begins with some residual beliefs, he discovers that any attempt to conform to the patterns bequeathed to his culture by the long-gone humans will fail. Whereas Stapledon allows some of the civilizations in *Last and First Men* to build on the accomplishments of previous ones, every movement into the past becomes for Lobey a dead-end. Consider Lobey's attempt to procure information about his lost Friza from the computer PHAEDRA; all that she can tell him is that he's in the wrong maze, the wrong myth, a human myth that cannot sustain him in his more complex and different present. Interestingly, the labyrinth in which Lobey finds PHAEDRA twice delivers him to essentially the same point, his starting point of confused loss and sorrow over Friza's death. This pattern of return is what Douglas Hofstadter calls a "strange loop," like a path in an Escher drawing that leads through impossible perspectives back to the initial level. Hofstadter talks about strange loops in relation not just to Escher but also to Bach and Gödel, a useful fact because Delany, too, refers to Gödel in discussing the Einstein intersection, the point at which old-style human beings departed and the different ones entered, the point at which dialectics and mediation merge, the point at which traditional logic fails. It is not enough to call this point one of paradox, as Stapledon might, or as the sign of some ineffable truth. The "strange loop" signals a different universe, not a more transcendent one.

Obviously, the world in which Delany writes is shot through with the assumptions of philosophical deconstruction, notions about undecidability, the replacement of logocentric linearity with semiotic slippage, and deferral of resolution or meaning. Stapledon's Modernism pushes hard against paradox toward the world of strange loops and difference. His philosophically informed penetration of thought systems, his attention to ideological conventionality, and his questioning of both self and language are all themes being worked out in intense detail by contemporary philosophers and cultural critics. *The Einstein Intersection* displays representatively the fruits for contemporary science fiction of the ground covered (and cleared) by Stapledon. Certainly the utopian thrust of this earlier work, its straining toward enlightened community, finds echoes in what Tom Moylan has called the "critical utopias" of Delany, Russ, and other science fiction greats. Delany's world, in its constant questioning of all assumptions and in its commitment to difference, obviously gestures toward an ideal world that has not yet been imagined. But the enabling, bracing speculations that mark the best of postmodern science fiction were made possible by Stapledon's multileveled probing of the paradoxes blocking his world's achievement of communal enlightenment.

NOTES

1. Smith calls this trait "dispassionate objectivity." Similarly, John Huntington comments on the Last Man's speaking "of appalling disasters and atrocities in an even voice." He goes on to discuss the "consistent irony that at times verges on comic understatement" in *Last and First Men* (Huntington, 354).

2. Stapledon readily admits to the vagueness of the term "spirit," but he defines it as follows: "The spirit is that in a man . . . in virtue of which he recognizes that a certain temper of experience and action, in fact a certain way of living, is right and beautiful absolutely. It is also that power in him by which, though precariously and intermittently, he actually lives in this way" (*Isms* 24).

3. For information on Dante and Stapledon, see McCarthy, 76–77. For discussion of Blake and Stapledon, see Bailey, 58–61 and 65.

4. For interesting commentary on the theme of linguistic inadequacy in Stapledon, see Branham, 255, who calls this feature the "self-deprecation" of Stapledon's style and praises his stylistic solution to the problem of joining "agnostic doubt to mystical vision."

5. Delany, 120, is worth quoting at some length here. Spider begins to explain difference in this way: "It isn't telepathy; it's not telekinesis—though both are chance phenomena that increase as difference increases. Lobey, Earth, the world, fifth planet from the sun—the species that stands on two legs and roams this thin wet crest: it's changing, Lobey. It's not the same. . . . We have taken over their abandoned world, and something new is happening to the fragments, something we can't even define with mankind's leftover vocabulary. You must take its importance exactly as that: it is indefinable; you are involved in it; it is wonderful, fearful, deep, ineffable to your explanations, opaque to your efforts to see through it." Here, Delany strikes me as protesting too much; difference as he narratizes it is not as ineffable as all that, and Delany is much less thematically concerned than Stapledon is to emphasize the limitations of his own descriptive abilities.

WORKS CITED

Bailey, K. V. "A Prized Harmony: Myth, Symbol and Dialectic in the Novels of Olaf Stapledon." *Foundation* 15 (1979): 53–66.

Branham, Robert. "Stapledon's 'Agnostic Mysticism.'" *Science-Fiction Studies* 9 (1982): 249–56.

Delany, Samuel R. *The Einstein Intersection*. New York: Bantam, 1967.

Hofstadter, Douglas R. *Gödel, Escher, Bach: An Eternal Golden Braid*. New York: Basic, 1979.

Huntington, John. "Olaf Stapledon and the Novel about the Future." *Contemporary Literature* 22 (Summer 1981): 349–65.

McCarthy, Patrick A. *Olaf Stapledon*. Boston: Twayne Publishers, 1982.

Moylan, Tom. *Demand the Impossible: Science Fiction and the Utopian Imagination*. New York: Methuen, 1987.

Smith, Curtis C. "Olaf Stapledon's Dispassionate Objectivity." In *Voices for the Future: Essays on Major Science Fiction Writers*, ed. Thomas D. Clareson. Bowling Green, Ohio: Bowling Green University Popular Press, 1976.

3

Stapledon and Literary Modernism

Patrick A. McCarthy

Olaf Stapledon's fictional writing resists simple categorization: it is often classed as science fiction or as utopian literature, but a careful reading of such works as *Last and First Men*, *Star Maker*, or *The Flames* reveals the inadequacy of these descriptive terms. As we might expect of the author of a book entitled *Beyond the "Isms"*, Stapledon's relationship to the various "isms" of the modern world is equally elusive, although critics have often attempted to pin him down to a single political, philosophical, or aesthetic creed. Before launching into my exposition, therefore, I should say that I intend to prove neither that Stapledon was a Modernist nor that he was anti-Modernist; instead, I hope to show that while Stapledon's works were certainly not typical Modernist productions, and while he objected to some aspects of Modernist literary practice and to the political conservatism that underlay it, Stapledon was in some key respects closer to the major Modernists than he would have expected.

Certainly he was more sympathetic to Modernism than we would assume from a reading of Leslie Fiedler's book, *Olaf Stapledon: A Man Divided*. Fiedler writes that "Stapledon remained oddly untouched by the whole adventure of Modernism, the subversion of the traditional concepts of character, narrative, and coherence" (35), and that, along with H. G. Wells, Stapledon "wrote as if neither the Modernist 'revolution of the word' nor the consequent splitting of literature into high and low, popular and elite had ever occurred" (40). At another point Fiedler adopts more extreme terms, claiming that Stapledon and his friend L. H. Myers "remained always hostile to Modernism" and "hated with especial virulence 'Bloomsbury'..."(38). Fiedler even goes so far as to say that Stapledon was particularly disturbed by James Joyce and to compare Stapledon's critique of Modernism with "the orthodox 'Stalinist' condemnation of the bourgeois avant-garde" (150–51).

If Stapledon were as "baffled" and alienated by Modernism as Fiedler believes, it is hard to imagine why the bibliography to *Waking World* (1934)—a sort of list of recommended reading—includes Joyce's *Ulysses*, D. H. Lawrence's *Letters*, the *Works*—otherwise undifferentiated—of Virginia Woolf, T. S. Eliot's *The Waste Land*, and I. A. Richards' *Principles of Literary Criticism* and *Practical Criticism*. Although the pages of *Waking World* contain no direct reference to any of these writers, it is intriguing to speculate on the possibility that Stapledon's reading of Joyce, Eliot, and Woolf might have had some influence on his statement that "In artistic experience we learn... to look at the world from a new angle, or with new eyes, and to enjoy it in an entirely new manner" (*WW* 86–87). This description of the function of art is as true of Stapledon's best productions as it is of the major examples of Modernist fiction and poetry.

Fiedler's analysis depends largely on the concept of Modernism as a form of literary "elitism" (8–9) associated with experiments in technique. Of course, as Irving Howe has observed, "formal experiment may frequently be a consequence or corollary of modernism, but its presence is not a sufficient condition for seeing a writer or a work as modernist" (22). Still, we would do well to remember that in their own way, Stapledon's works are experimental—even radically so. In a 1924 letter to *Poetry*, Stapledon defended "those who say they are tired of orthodox rhyme and metre," arguing that their complaint is not against form but against the kind of formalism that entails the adoption of traditional forms out of laziness. Although he carefully limited his comments to experiments with rhyme and related sound effects, Stapledon's interest in developing new literary forms is quite in keeping with the fact that he was writing at the height of the Modernist period, the time when formal experimentation of all kinds was especially popular among writers and avant-garde critics, if not with the average reader.

Consider a more obvious mode of experimentation: the writer's struggle against the idea of the "novel." Recognizing how little the term "novel" could mean if the category included *Finnegans Wake*, Harry Levin instead placed Joyce's final book in the "class of unclassifiable books," where it resides in the company of "*The Anatomy of Melancholy*, *Don Juan*, *Sartor Resartus*, *Moby-Dick*, and *The Golden Bough*" (165). Virginia Woolf realized that she, too, was composing something other than "novels," for we find her writing in her diary, in June 1925, "I have an idea that I will invent a new name for my books to supplant 'novel'. A new ——— by Virginia Woolf. But what?

Elegy?" (Vol. 3, 34). The novel was a construct whose form could be taken for granted, but what Woolf and Joyce were writing was a kind of prose fiction in which every formal element needed to be created to meet the demands of the writer's theme.

Now, this is a dilemma that Stapledon would have understood, for he faced it himself in his more ambitious projects. In the Preface to *Last and First Men* he comments on the book's narrative perspective, which violates our conventional notions of space and time by having the book narrated directly to us by one of the Last Men living on Neptune some two billion years in the future: "only by some such radical and bewildering device," he says, "could I embody the possibility that there may be more in time's nature than is revealed to us. Indeed, only by some such trick could I do justice to the conviction that our whole present mentality is but a confused and halting first experiment" (*LFM* Preface:10). Note here the typical Modernist insistence that form and content are inseparable. If Stapledon's fiction contains "few experiments with shifting points of view or with the direct rendition of consciousness through language," as I have observed (146), it certainly includes some daring experiments with narrative perspective and fictional structure. The prefaces to later books are even more explicit in their rejection of conventional narrative form. In *Last Men in London* (1932), Stapledon writes, "though this is a work of fiction, it does not pretend to be a novel.... There is no plot, except the theme of man's struggle in this awkward age to master himself and to come to terms with the universe" (*LML* Preface:9). In *Star Maker* (1937), he declares, "judged by the standards of the Novel [the book] is remarkably bad. In fact, it is no novel at all" (*SM* Preface:250). Likewise, *Death into Life* begins with a prefatory note consisting of the flat declaration that "this fantasy is not a novel." The genre of Stapledon's posthumously published books, *The Opening of the Eyes* and *4 Encounters*, is even more in doubt, each of these works being *sui generis*.

As Howe's comment suggests, though, technical experimentation is primarily the by-product of an altered vision that is at the heart of the Modernist mode. Virginia Woolf's famous comment that human nature changed sometime around December 1910 is one of the many signs that Modernist writers felt that traditional answers, traditional means of describing reality, no longer sufficed. One of the symptoms of Modernism is a sense of alienation or discontinuity, caused in part by the accelerated rate of change in all aspects of human life. Malcolm Bradbury has remarked that the "sense of intensified crisis" in modern literature is related to "the knowledge that change is disturbing and upsetting the conditions of thought and art themselves" (40). The Modernists find in twentieth-century life a radical discontinuity, a loss of connection that implies a loss of meaning; and they attempt to create, or forge, a connection between the isolated individual and something else—another person, as in *To the Lighthouse*; another culture, as in *A Passage to India*; the heroic past, as in *The Waste Land*; or all three, as in *Ulysses*. The epigraph to *Howards End*—"Only connect . . . "—emphasizes this aspect of Modernism while Pound's dictum, "make it new," stresses the artist's duty to discover an appropriate rhythm, image, or form for his theme.

I would like to comment on three aspects of Modernism that are related to this sense of radical historical discontinuity, and to suggest that in all three cases there is some affinity between Stapledon's work and the more typically Modernist mode. First, there is the anti-historicism of much of modern literature, which tends to reject notions of progress or development insofar as the historical process determines the nature, value, or significance of human life. Second, there is the substitution of aestheticism for historicism as the primary model of order and coherence; thus the work is seen largely on its own terms and, in the most extreme cases, is regarded as self-sufficient. Finally, there is a tendency for art to become its own subject, so that literary works become increasingly reflexive or self-referential.

Among the devices that Modernist writers use to escape from the tyranny of history are the transcendent moment and the mythological cycle. The transcendent moment may take the form of Hopkins' experience of "inscape," Joyce's "epiphany," Woolf's "moments of being," the escape into the rose garden in Eliot's "Burnt Norton," or any other attempt to discover the eternal within the temporal, the visionary within the mundane; the mythic cycle replaces linear historical progress most obviously in Joyce's *Finnegans Wake*, but also in Pound's *Cantos* and Eliot's *The Waste Land*. Eliot stated the case for the "mythical method"—as opposed to the "narrative method"—in fiction when he said, in a review of *Ulysses*, that Joyce's development of "a continuous parallel between contemporaneity and antiquity . . . is simply a way of controlling, of ordering, of giving a shape and a significance to the immense panorama of futility and anarchy which is contemporary history" (177).

In historical terms, Stapledon's works generally operate on two levels. There is of course a sense of historical engagement, even urgency: in the preface to *Last and First Men*, for example, Stapledon says that he has "tried to make the story relevant to the change that is taking place today in man's outlook," and in the prefaces to *Star Maker* and *Darkness and the Light* he feels compelled to apologize for writing what some writers might regard as a waste of paper or, at best a "distraction." Moreover, the extended analysis, in *Last Men in London*, of the origins of World War I is surely an attempt to place the modern mentality within the context of a particular historical and evolutionary process, while the future histories of *Last and First Men* and *Darkness and the Light* offer Stapledon great opportunities to concentrate on historical development at the expense of the more typically Modernist focus on individual life. Even the protagonists of *Odd John* and *Sirius*, who receive what is for Stapledon a very thorough development of individual character, are seen primarily as by-products or exempla of evolutionary processes, so that they exist within a very clearly defined biological and historical context.

At the same time—and with Stapledon there is always an "at the same time"—in these novels, the study of the temporal is generally important not for its own sake but as a means of gaining entree to the eternal. In fact, to be entirely wrapped up in the present moment is to lose the heightened perspective that Stapledon always sought—what the narrator of *Last Men in London* calls a "Neptunian" perspective. Moreover, the historical focus of *Last and First Men* is itself subverted by the narrative strategies adopted in that novel, for as John Huntington has shown, "the important sequence of the novel is not that of history or even that of the progress of humanity's higher stages, but rather the baffling order of awarenesses that the narrator (rather than history itself) imposes on the reader. Any suggestion of historical pattern that may emerge is either shattered by an unexpected and unpredictable event which leaves 'mere continuity' as the only order possible, or rendered trivial by the narrator's compressons and elisions" (353–54). This emphasis on the disorientation of the reader is surprisingly similar to the tactics adopted often in modern poetry and fiction, where the intent is to undermine the reader's comfortable relationship to the text—a relationship made more comfortable by the notions of historical progress that Stapledon rejects. Indeed, the purely time-bound or historical viewpoint is an aspect of the mental slumber that Stapledon describes at the opening of *Last and First Men* and that he refers to in key sections of *Star Maker* and other books. Its converse is the "awakening" of the human—and later the cosmic—spirit into a detached, almost divine, perspective. This is Stapledon's nearest equivalent to the epiphanic moment in Joyce, the moment at which the individual object is stabilized in the imagination so that its form appears "radiant" and eternal; but whereas Joyce stresses the perception of a common object or event, Stapledon aims at the total form of the spirit in both its evolving and its completed aspects.

One of the more telling connections between Stapledon and Joyce lies in this association of artistic experience with the revelation of the eternal. In Joyce, the connection between god and artist is stated most explicitly in *A Portrait of the Artist as a Young Man*, where Stephen Dedalus compares the mature dramatic artist to "the god of the creation, [who] remains within or behind or above his handiwork, invisible, refined out of existence, paring his fingernails" (215). The indifference of Joyce's artist-god toward his creation is echoed in Stapledon's portrayal of the Star Maker as a cosmic artist who creates successive cosmoses out of his own potential and then dispassionately evaluates his own creations. Moreover, the narrator, in his role as the cosmic spirit, momentarily achieves a "surprising angle of vision" corresponding to the eternal and detached perspective of the Star Maker, so that in viewing the creation and destruction of our cosmos he can rise above the viewpoint of human, and even cosmic, history (*SM* 15:423).

This is by no means the only passage in which Stapledon pushes the analogy between divine and artistic creation, for several other characters or groups in his books view human or cosmic history in aesthetic terms. In *Last and First Men*, for example, the Third Men regard music both as the highest expression of the spirit and as the ultimate form of reality, and the book concludes with a speech by one of the Last Men who describes mankind as a kind of music that is not merely ephemeral but triumphs over time to become "eternally a beauty in the eternal form of things" (*LFM* 16:246). The attitude expressed here is similar to the one that Stapledon recommends to us in a section of *Waking World* entitled "The Analogy of Art," where he expounds upon the idea that our response to the cosmos ought to be like that of the spectator at a play who "cares most about the play *as a play*":

> I do not mean that he is interested to see how far and in what manner it fulfils the formal principles of dramatic art, but that he *feels* the play as a whole. If the spirit of the play is tragic, he wants it to fulfil its tragic nature. Although at the same time he grieves for the suffering persons, he delights in the terrible relentless way in which the opening situation of the play develops into the final tragedy. He recognizes that if *this* play had ended happily after all, it would not have been true to itself. (*WW* 222)

Stapledon's search for aesthetic analogies for life and history suggests an attitude at least compatible with the Modernist tendency that José Ortega y Gasset has described as the "dehumanization of art"—the tendency to reverse the traditional relationship between art and life by refusing to regard the art work merely as a representative of life. Shakespeare tells us that art holds the mirror up to life, but modern writers more often regard life itself, or our understanding of it, as in some way dependent upon the conventions and formulae of art. As a result, Modernist art generally refuses to pose as what it obviously is not—life—and instead calls attention to its status as art. In modern literature this may be accomplished by any of a number of strategies that we have come to call "reflexive" or "self-referential," for example by focusing on the process through which the writer came to develop into the person who wrote the book or by taking as its subject an analogous aesthetic problem like the one faced by the painter Lily Briscoe in *To the Lighthouse*. Discussions of modern literature as reflexive can of course be exaggerated to the point of absurdity if they are taken to mean, for example, that a novel like *Remembrance of Things Past* forms a closed system with no reference to the outside world; but there is a consistent tendency for Modernist works to turn back upon themselves and to refer in some way to their status as literary artifacts.

How does this tendency manifest itself in Stapledon's works? Most obviously, perhaps, one might point to the narrative pattern in *Star Maker*, a book in which three searches culminate in a great moment of vision. There is the individual narrator's search for a fundamental principle that will lend significance to human life; the search of the "cosmic mind," of which the narrator ultimately becomes part, for its creator; and the Star Maker's search for self-fulfillment through a kind of artistic expression. Robert Crossley has called attention to a lecture note which Stapledon wrote while preparing to discuss his own book. The note reads, "fiction of the Maker—artist," and Crossley astutely observes that this phrase "suggests that the author wanted to look at his masterpiece not primarily as a theological romance but as a self-reflective parable about the nature of creativity in which the visionary spectacle of the star maker's drafting and redrafting of the universe becomes a macrocosmic emblem of the human artist's repeated struggle to achieve satsifying forms" (37). Note here, too, that the universe becomes a self-contained whole, conceived and judged in aesthetic terms but ultimately developing its own values and, in a sense, facing and judging its maker. Moreover, we are given not a direct account of the Star Maker but a kind of fiction: as the cosmic mind the narrator has a vision of the Star Maker but is unable to recall it, remembering only "a fantastic reflex of [the vision], an echo, a symbol, a myth, a crazy dream" that he relates to us (*SM* 14:412). That art achieves a life of its own is not a peculiarly modern idea—the myth of Pygmalion and Galatea comes readily to mind—but there is something very modern in Stapledon's conception of the way the cosmic spirit develops myths of its own creation, in effect turning the Star Maker into a fictional character in order to understand its own being. We need to remind ourselves that the Star Maker was *already* a fictional character to see how thoroughly reflexive and paradoxical this fiction has become.

Two other aspects of the book's reflexivity are prominent in its cosmic vision. One is Stapledon's characteristic concern with perspective, a subject that he handles with unusual sophistication throughout *Star Maker*. The narrator, in fact, describes himself early in the book as "disembodied, wandering view-point" (*SM* 2:268), and he frequently alludes to the complex narrative perspective of a book in which the narrator is both an individual and a group mind (e.g., *SM* 8:343–45). When the narrator describes the creation of his own cosmos—the one "which contains the readers and the writer of this book" (*SM* 15:422)—he emphasizes the perspective from which he viewed, and now relates, the event:

> Although this new cosmos was my own cosmos, I regarded it from a surprising angle of vision. No longer did it appear as a familiar sequence of historical events beginning with the initial physical explosion and advancing to the final death. I saw it now not from within the flux of the cosmical time but quite otherwise. I watched the fashioning of the cosmos in the time proper to the Star Maker; and the sequence of the Star Maker's creative acts was very different from the sequence of historical events. (*SM* 15:423)

Note that this "surprising angle of vision" involves a typically Modernist rejection of historical sequence as well as an approximation of the Star Maker's own viewpoint, which is that of eternity.

The other Modernist tendency that I see in the narrator's description of his vision is the emphasis on the nature and limitations of the language in which the book is described. This, of course, is an aspect of point of view: every language contains within it cultural assumptions and biases that allow us only to describe experiences within the framework allowed by a particular culture. Moreover, certain experiences are beyond human language altogether—as Dante found at the end of the *Paradiso*. In the description of the Other Earth, Stapledon calls attention to the arbitrary and limited nature of all language when he emphasizes the predominance of gustatory metaphors in the Other Men's language in place of the visual metaphors that we find throughout our language: our "brilliant" becomes their "tasty," while "for 'lucid' they would use a term which in primitive times was employed by hunters to signify an easily runnable taste-trail" (*SM* 3:275). In the later chapters, we also find references to the language in which the book is written—that is, to the terms in which it is conceived and experienced. Stapledon warns against the dangers of anthropomorphism in his description of the mentality of stars even while conceding that "it is impossible to speak of their experience in any other terms" (*SM* 11:388); soon thereafter, he repeats that "to describe the mentality of stars is of course to describe the unintelligible by means of intelligible but falsifying human metaphors" (*SM* 11:391). The impossibility of describing nonhuman or superhuman experiences in a human language is a familiar one in Stapledon's books, as the problem of constructing a "true" account becomes part of the account.

Star Maker's composition is not, of course, its primary subject matter, but it is one of the subjects that constantly intrude upon the narrative. Another aspect of this reflexivity is Stapledon's tendency to represent the book explicitly as a book. The Time Scales of *Last and First Men* and *Star Maker* call attention to the book's reality as a product of print technology, and thereby contribute to its status as what Ortega calls "artistic" art; they also help to provide much of the "spatial form" that Joseph Frank has shown is central to modern fiction and poetry, by treating the book's temporal action as something that can be rendered directly in spatial terms. The fictional introductions to *Last and First Men*, *Last Men in London*, and *The Flames*, and the Note on Magnitude appended to *Star Maker*, are further examples of Stapledon's determination to avoid the conventions of realism and present his writing to us directly as writing.

I think it is clear that Stapledon was sensitive to the conditions that gave rise to Modernism, and that the techniques and vision of his books show, at times, an affinity to those of his more famous contemporaries. Yet Stapledon remained always his own man, and his responses to Modernism include a healthy dose of skepticism about its aims and means. Fiedler reports that at the Wrocław conference in 1948 Stapledon defended T. S. Eliot against an intemperate attack by the Soviet keynote speaker, Alexander Fadayev: in response to Fadayev's implied comparison of Eliot, O'Neill, Sartre, and Malraux to jackals and hyenas, Stapledon called attention to Eliot's importance and noted that "both sides, not just one, were guilty of using 'instruments which pervert the truth' " (23). This, however, is a defense that suggests little more than qualified admiration for Eliot. A somewhat more positive assessment of Eliot's poetry is contained in Stapledon's unpublished paper "Thoughts on the Modern Spirit," (2) which Crossley believes was composed during the period 1932–1935. The remarks on Eliot are made in the context of Stapledon's elaboration on the mood of "disinterested admiration" for the universe, a mood that obviously resembles Stapledon's own attitude in his works at the time. I cite in full Stapledon's remarks on Eliot:

> I would hazard the guess that the work of Mr. T. S. Eliot is inspired by this admiration of an objective world whose form involves both good and evil. Mr. I. A. Richards, I know, argues that such writing is concerned solely to make a "music of ideas"; but in this view he is perhaps prejudiced by his own theory of value and of the nature of art in general. It would seem more true to say that Mr. Eliot calls forth or indicates a music of objective characters. Or perhaps with more strictness we should say that he constructs symbols which are indeed themselves "music of ideas," but in their music they purport to symbolise or epitomise the music of the spheres. This is perhaps the nerve of the matter. In disillusion, we may sometimes discover, or seem to ourselves to discover, an unlooked-for music of facts. And whatever be the true epistemology of value it is very important to inspect clearly the deliverance of such experiences. (21–22)

This discussion, whatever its value as an analysis of Eliot's ideas, is obviously sympathetic to his poetry. Although it was definitely written after Eliot's conversion to the Church of England (1927), and almost certainly after the publication of "Ash Wednesday" (1930), the paper gives no hint of Stapledon's unease at Eliot's move from the disillusion of the *Waste Land* period to religious orthodoxy. By 1944, however, when he published *Sirius*, Stapledon was clearly unhappy with the direction Eliot had taken. His dissatisfaction is expressed in the description of Sirius's readings in "the poetry of self and universe":

> Hardy at one time fascinated him. The early Eliot intoxicated him with new rhythms and with a sense of facing the worst in preparation for a new vision. But the vision never came. Instead came orthodoxy. Sirius longed for that vision. He hoped for it from the younger moderns; but though he was even younger than any of them, they meant little to him. (*Sirius* 6:218)

Here, it seems to me, Sirius is assessing Eliot in much the same way as Stapledon did: as an innovative writer whose poetry finally promised more than it delivered, possibly because he lacked the courage to continue to face life without the prop of organized religion. What is important to note here is that there is no reaction against Modernism *per se*; if anything, Stapledon criticizes Eliot for failing to carry through, for falling back upon conventional and traditional solutions to problems that require a thoroughly modern response.

A stronger and more hostile criticism of modern literature occurs in *Odd John*, where John derides "the bright young things of literature and art [who] set out to enjoy themselves as best they might in a crashing world" (*OJ* 10:65). Here the attack is aimed at the Bloomsbury Group, whose reputation for sexual bohemianism and whose emphasis on aesthetic and intellectual pleasure John regards as forms of self-indulgence and, ultimately, self-hatred. John gives the Bloomsbury set a prominence and influence far greater than that which it ever enjoyed, referring to its members as "the leaders of thought, or leaders of fashion in thought," and calling the whole group "the centre to which nearly all the best sensibility and best intellect of the country gets attracted in the expectation of meeting its kind and enriching its experience"; but he finds the group "a web, a subtle mesh of convention" that entraps its adherents in a useless round of superficial experiences even while giving them the illusion of their own freedom. The whole idea of Bloomsbury, John declares, is based upon the avoidance of real experience and the substitution for it of "all sorts of minor and superficial (though sensational) experiences" (*OJ* 10:66). Although John is talking specifically about the lives of the Bloomsburyites, presumably he is also describing the motives and nature of their literary and artistic productions.

Taken out of context, the passage might well be used to justify Leslie Fiedler's grand declaration that Stapledon "hated [the Bloomsbury Group] with especial virulence" (38). This assessment, however, depends upon a fairly straightforward equation of John's views with Stapledon's, and there are reasons to suppose that, instead, we should regard the narrator of *Odd John*—a journalist whom John insists on calling "Fido"—as the character whose views most closely approximate Stapledon's. Thus it is worth citing the paragraph that follows John's indictment of Bloomsbury:

> This analysis made me uncomfortable [says the narrator], for though I was not one of "them" I could not disguise from myself that the same sort of condemnation might apply to me. John evidently saw my thoughts, for he grinned, and moreover indulged in an entirely vulgar wink. Then he said, "Strikes home, old thing, doesn't it? Never mind, you're not *in* the web. You're an outsider. Fate has kept you safely fluttering in the backward North." (*OJ* 10:66)

Here we have Stapledon's rather ironic description of his own situation as "an outsider" living in "the backward North," far from the social and intellectual center of English life. The narrator's self-deprecating tone is typical of Stapledon, whose modesty stands in sharp contrast to John's arrogance; if we take the narrator to be a portrait of Stapledon, the passage implies that he is not any better than the Bloomsbury writers, merely less encumbered by the cultural environment that both contributes to the prominence of Bloomsbury and ensnares it in a web of unperceived conventions.

The discussion of Bloomsbury in *Odd John* focuses on extra-literary matters, but in *Last Men in London* there is a passage which Fiedler (89–90) seems correct in regarding as an analysis of the Bloomsbury set. Here, the criticism is that these "artists, despisers of the mere analytical intelligence," have so made a cult of art that for them, "love and hate and life itself [are] but the matter of art," while "the whole meaning of human existence [seems] to lie solely in the apprehension of forms intrinsically 'significant,' and in the embodiment of visions without relevance" (*LML* 8:237). The retreat from the world, and from "relevance," is what Stapledon finds objectionable in the works of these "Microcosmic creators"; the problem is not that the writers have erred in their attempt to assimilate human experience into an appropriate aesthetic form, but that "the very intensity of their single aesthetic achievement" tends to deprive it of practical significance. And for Stapledon, literature ultimately must have some relevance to the fundamental problems of life.

Since the most prominent writer who was truly a central figure in the Bloomsbury Group was Virginia Woolf, it is worth noting that the brief correspondence between Stapledon and Woolf indicates that the two authors found reason to praise one another's work—although Woolf, in her diary, admitted the possibility that she was "more genially disposed" to Stapledon because he had said he admired her work (Woolf V, 99). When Stapledon sent her a copy of *Star Maker*, Woolf responded with a letter in which she noted that "sometimes it seems to me that you are grasping ideas that I have tried to express, much more fumblingly, in fiction. But you have gone much further, & I can't help envying you—as one does those who reach what one has aimed at" (Crossley 29). Exactly which of the ideas in *Star Maker* Virginia Woolf found appealing is a matter for conjecture, although a diary entry later the same month indicates that Stapledon had praised Woolf's 1937 novel *The Years*, so that perhaps she was attracted by the fact that Stapledon had achieved on the large scale the sort of cosmic perspective that she attempted in parts of that book.

It is clear that Stapledon's response to literary Modernism was complex and ambivalent. On the other hand, he was inclined to adopt aesthetic models for individual and cosmic life; on the other hand, he was wary of writers who seemed to value artistic form more than human experience, personal expression above intelligibility. His essay "Literature and the Unity of Man" is significant in this regard. There, Stapledon considers the argument that depth of personal experience is more important than the accessibility of the literary work, and admits that Joyce's *Ulysses* and Dante's *Divine Comedy* draw much of their strength from their accumulation of local and personal references, but he finds that the "direct contribution to human unity" of much of modern literature is "very slight" because the works are little more than "pregnant cross-word puzzles" (114–15).

There is no reference, in this essay, to *Finnegans Wake*, which had appeared two years earlier (1939) in its final form, after a decade and a half during which parts were published separately under the general title *Work in Progress*. Despite two features that are reminiscent of Stapledon's own work—the structural and thematic use of mythic cycles and the attempt to achieve a perspective which is both personal and all-encompassing—*Finnegans Wake* is unlikely to have proved very attractive to Stapledon, who would have objected to the obstacles to understanding posed by Joyce's experimentation in style and narrative development. *Finnegans Wake* is probably the most extreme example of one aspect of Modernism, its tendency to develop meaning through a complex set of interwoven allusions and other motifs; and this characteristic often limits the reading audience to those with the training, the inclination, and sufficient free time to work through the difficulties of a particular novel or poem. Thus it would have to be said of *Finnegans Wake*, as Stapledon said of other modern works, that "excellent as this kind of literature is in itself... its direct contribution to human unity must at present be very slight" (115).

Ironically, however, Modernism is itself strongly biased toward, and influenced by, internationalism, so much so that Hugh Kenner (16) excludes Virginia Woolf from the Modernist club on the grounds that she is only "a twentieth-century English novelist of manners" who has adopted some techniques from real Modernists like Joyce, Eliot, and Pound, expatriates who broke sharply with the literary traditions of their homelands and with English literary practice, learning more from continental writers than from literature in their native language. If *Ulysses* and *Finnegans Wake* have had little direct influence on the progress toward human unity, perhaps it might fairly be asked which books have had this desired effect. More to the point, the Modernists scorned nationalism and parochialism just as much as Stapledon did: Irish readers might have a better feel than others for the setting of *Ulysses*, but part of the book's appeal lies precisely in its violation of national cultural boundaries. To achieve a perspective outside the limitations of a particular time and place is the Modernist dream, and it is one that Stapledon shared.

Perhaps I have overstated my case, overlooking factors that separate Stapledon from the Modernists. Politically, Stapledon stood well to the left of most of the Modernists, who ranged from the fascist Pound to the mandarin socialists of Bloomsbury; stylistically, he had more in common with Victorian than with modern writers. Yet if Modernism had relatively little direct influence on Stapledon, he shared with its practitioners central assumptions about the nature and function of art—assumptions that Cyril Connolly has summarized eloquently in his statement that "the value of Picasso's *Guernica*, of the work of Proust, of the landscapes of Cezanne, is to penetrate the darkness which surrounds the human camp fire, and reveal something of the landscape beyond it" (125). That attempt to penetrate the darkness is what gives to Stapledon's work—as to that of Joyce, Eliot, Woolf, Mann, and the other great Modernists—its true and lasting significance.

WORKS CITED

Bradbury, Malcolm. *The Social Context of Modern English Literature*. New York: Schocken Books, 1971.

Connolly, Cyril. "Writers & Society 1940–3." In *The Selected Essays of Cyril Connolly*, ed. Peter Quennell. New York: Persea Books, 1984.

Crossley, Robert. "Olaf Stapledon and the Idea of Science Fiction." *Modern Fiction Studies* 32 (Spring 1986): 21–42.

Eliot, T. S. "*Ulysses*, Order, and Myth." In *Selected Prose of T. S. Eliot*, ed. Frank Kermode. New York: Harcourt Brace Jovanovich and Farrar, Straus and Giroux, 1975.

Fiedler, Leslie A. *Olaf Stapledon: A Man Divided*. New York: Oxford University Press, 1983.

Frank, Joseph. "Spatial Form in Modern Literature." In *The Widening Gyre: Crisis and Mastery in Modern Literature*. New Brunswick: Rutgers University Press, 1963.

Howe, Irving. "The Idea of the Modern." In *The Idea of the Modern in Literature and the Arts*, ed. Irving Howe. New York: Horizon Press, 1967.

Huntington, John. "Olaf Stapledon and the Novel about the Future." *Contemporary Literature* 22 (Summer 1981): 349–65.

Joyce, James. *A Portrait of the Artist as a Young Man*, ed. Chester G. Anderson. New York: Viking Critical Library, 1968.

Kenner, Hugh. *A Colder Eye: The Modern Irish Writers*. New York: Alfred A. Knopf, 1983.

Levin, Harry. *James Joyce: A Critical Introduction*. 1941; revised ed., New York: New Directions, 1960.

McCarthy, Patrick A. *Olaf Stapledon*. Boston: Twayne Publishers, 1982.

Ortega y Gasset, José. "The Dehumanization of Art." In *The Dehumanization of Art and Other Essays on Art, Culture, and Literature*. Princeton: Princeton University Press, 1968.

Stapledon, Olaf. "Literature and the Unity of Man." In *Writers in Freedom: A Symposium*, ed. Herman Ould. London: Hutchinson, [1942].

———. "Rhyme, Assonance and Vowel Contrast." *Poetry* 7, no. 65 (August-September 1924): 194–96.

———. "Thoughts on the Modern Spirit." Typescript prepared by Robert Crossley from Stapledon's manuscript.

Woolf, Virginia. *The Dairy of Virginia Woolf*, ed. Anne Olivier Bell. Volume 3, 1925–1930. New York: Harcourt Brace Jovanovich, 1980. Volume 5, 1936—1941. New York: Harcourt Brace Jovanovich, 1984.

4

"Seeing It Whole": Olaf Stapledon and the Issue of Totality

Charles Elkins

Olaf Stapledon's place in the literary history of science fiction is assured; he stands out as one of the four or five most influential writers in the genre. His specific contributions are detailed by many very good critical articles and at least three full-length studies.[1] For these reasons and for those that I will try to explain in the next few paragraphs, this essay is not an attempt at another celebration or interpretation of any of Stapledon's works, particularly of *Last and First Men* or *Star Maker*, the two future histories upon which I concentrate. Indeed, in a couple of senses, this is not a critical article at all, if by that adjective one means a reading which attempts to discern some overall unity or pattern in Stapledon's works or that seeks to resolve the myriad contradictions and tensions within a single work or within the evolution of Stapledon's thoughts. If we as critics have learned nothing else in the last few years, it should be that such projects are essentially futile. Literary works by their very nature resist the stability and unity that we wish to impose upon them.

I believe this to be a particularly appropriate stance for studying Stapledon's fiction. It is not simply that his works defy any definitive interpretation, but in attempting to create one the critic would be caught in the same trap within which Stapledon found himself as he strove to interpret reality (human nature, history, society, nature, the cosmos, the absolute, etc.). That is to say, both projects—the critic's and Stapledon's—assume the need to understand the object of study in its totality and to see this particular totality—in the critic's case, the work; in Stapledon's case whatever aspect of reality he happened to be studying—in its relationship to the whole.

The problem is that one can never understand anything in its totality, and while it is common to say that "context" determines meaning, what are the boundaries of context?

It is this desire to overcome division and contradiction by attempting to assume a holistic perspective and the problems that one encounters in making this move that are the major concern of this essay. Rather than write another interpretation of Stapledon's work, I want to appropriate his future histories for my own purposes, to say something about Stapledon's project, his cosmic perspective, and to relate it to a similar project in Marxism—a philosophy and political movement to which Stapledon was very sympathetic—and, finally, to look at both Stapledon's cosmic perspective and Marxism's drive for totality in light of some post-structuralist considerations. The first two themes—the cosmic perspective and Marxism—are explicit in Stapledon's works; the third, post-structuralist criticism, can be used as a lens, one not traditionally employed in Stapledon criticism, to reveal some of the unresolved questions concerning the first two themes, questions that Stapledon struggled to resolve.

I should declare at the outset that I am not interested in trying to settle once and for all the degree to which Stapledon was or was not committed to Marxism. I am content to accept the general consensus that toward the end of his life he became disillusioned with the Bolsheviks and the Communist Party but that he was generally faithful to Marxism's general critique of capitalism and that he remained, at least philosophically, a socialist until he died.

Because it bears upon Stapledon's sense of being "divided" and his affinities with Matthew Arnold, one debate that does interest me, one that with Professor McCarthy's essay for this volume has taken on added importance, is Stapledon's relationship with Modernism. McCarthy takes issue with Leslie Fiedler's assertion that Stapledon was "untouched by the whole adventure of Modernism, the subversion of the traditional concepts of character, narrative, and coherence" (Fiedler 35). McCarthy demonstrates conclusively not only that Stapledon was influenced by Modernism but that many of his themes and literary strategies are analogous to and find echoes in the works of such indisputably Modernist writers as James Joyce and Virginia Woolf.

However, McCarthy understands (and makes the point in his book on Stapledon) that Fiedler is also correct in recognizing the late Victorian elements in Stapledon's work. McCarthy compares Stapledon's situation to that of Matthew Arnold. Like Matthew Arnold and his narrator in the poem "Stanzas from the Grande Chartreuse," Stapledon and many of his characters are also caught between "two worlds, one dead, / The other powerless to be born"

(McCarthy 51). Without embracing Arnold's elitism—although Stapledon's attitude toward the "masses" was often ambivalent—or Arnold's faith in the "saving remnant" (here, again, Stapledon is ambivalent), Stapledon's notion of the ideal civilization comes very close to Arnold's Hellenism. Further, Arnold's ideal of the critical attitude, his "disinterested objectivity," finds an echo in Stapledon's "dispassionate objectivity." Finally, Arnold's ideal of critical practice, "to see the object as it really is," is similar to Stapledon's attempt to understand man and his history, to understand (what by now has become a tired cliché) "the meaning of life" by trying to "see it whole."

Like many of his main characters, Stapledon does not quite fit into either historical period; he is temperamentally and literarily a transition figure. Fiedler and McCarthy have done admirable jobs in placing Stapledon in his historical and cultural milieu, especially that period between the world wars. What has been noted but not emphasized is Stapledon's relation to F. R. Leavis and the *Scrutiny* group. Readers acquainted with this journal, the biographies of Leavis and his wife, Queenie Dorothy Roth (i.e., Q. D. Leavis), and their views on literature, may be surprised to learn that Stapledon contributed to *Scrutiny*. While it is clear that he did not share their critical practice—he was not a critic—nor their political conservatism, there are a number of instances where Stapledon's thought and the *Scrutiny* group's cultural criticism parallel each other. Their thinking and attitudes toward the contemporary "situation" and their solutions—at least their literary solutions—for what they saw as a world in crisis are remarkably similar.

Literary historians have noted how F. R. Leavis assumed the mantle of Matthew Arnold and, at the same time, helped to usher in literary Modernism by promoting the works of such writers as D. H. Lawrence, James Joyce and T. S. Eliot. Like Arnold, the critics associated with *Scrutiny* saw literature as a substitute for religion, however that might be realized. As Terry Eagleton writes, literature was not only needed to " 'Hellenize' or cultivate the philistine middle class" (24), but was ideally suited to "carry through the ideological task which religion left off" (28). If Stapledon did not embrace literature as a substitute for religion, he believed that literature, as myth, could foster a religious *attitude* toward humanity and the cosmos.[2] Stapledon also saw literature's function, as did Arnold and Leavis, as a "criticism of life and partly a Joycean instrument for forging 'the uncreated conscience' of the species" (Crossley 296). In one of his essays for *Scrutiny*—"On Escapism in Literature"—Stapledon argues for the serious social function of literature: the function of literature is " 'to render experience cognitively more true and affective and conatively more appropriate.' Literature *clarifies* understanding by offering fresh views of familiar experience and it *develops* possibilities for action by adumbrating new modes of experience" (Crossley 296). Leavis insisted on the seriousness of literature; in fact, literature, especially English literature, was "*the* supremely civilizing spirit, the spiritual essence of the social formation" (Eagleton 31). Like Stapledon, the *Scrutiny* group saw civilization threatened by the "commercial spirit"—Stapledon was usually more blunt; he called it capitalism—and only the creative energies of literature could save it. Literature was to be the vehicle for putting man in touch with the "spirit" of civilization and helping him to transcend the petty, material concerns of the moment by refashioning his sensibilities. This project is very similar to Stapledon's desire to "awaken" man to the "spirit."

Like those at *Scrutiny*, T. S. Eliot was "repelled... by the spiritual barrenness of industrial capitalism" (Eagleton 38) and the culture it produced. Eliot countered this cultural wasteland by a wholesale revision of the literary canon, which Eagleton describes as an assault on "the whole ideology of middle class liberalism, the official ideology of industrial capitalist society" (39). For Eliot, "the crisis of European society—global war, severe class-conflict, failing capitalist economies—might be resolved by turning one's back on history altogether and putting mythology in its place" (Eagleton 41). Stapledon did not go this far, but as I have noted elsewhere, this desire to create myth—to give a sense of coherence and meaning to history—was very attractive to Stapledon.[3]

I mention Leavis, Eliot, and *Scrutiny* because, while there are important differences, they share with Stapledon many of the same views concerning the particular historical crisis within which they found themselves and concerning the social function of literature. Leavis, like Stapledon, was a transitional figure, caught between the aesthetics of the late Victorians and of Modernism. In many ways, like Stapledon, he succeeded in bridging both worlds; in some ways, like Stapledon, he failed.

I have previously taken Stapledon to task for his announced project—to write myth. I argued that Stapledon was not creating myth, and his attempt to do so violated some of the fundamental assumptions of science fiction. I still believe that I was essentially correct; however, I was thinking of myth in a particular way, especially as myth is opposed to fiction.[4] I was troubled by what I saw as Stapledon's affinity for Hegel and his almost Spenglerian attitude toward man and his history. I was thinking of myth in much the same way that Ernst Cassirer describes it. That is to say, myth is what *is*; it is *reality*, and to the degree that people become self-conscious about myth, it is no longer myth. Stapledon's attitude toward the human situation seemed to me similar to Leibniz's assertion that whatever is, is right—the philosophy satirized by Voltaire's *Candide*. This view is similar to Hegel's view that what is rational is real and what is real is rational. Cassirer, in one of his last essays, "Philosophy and Politics" (1944), concludes that Hegel's argument ends in a "new attitude":

> For now philosophical thought gives up all claims to reform the world, to mold it into a new shape. It becomes its highest and its only aim to understand and to interpret it—to describe the historical reality as it *is*, not what it ought to be. (226)

Cassirer connects Hegel's thought to Spengler's, particularly Spengler's *Decline of the West* (1918), where Spengler argues from necessity and fatality to reach the conclusion that the West is doomed.

And indeed, there is a strong Spenglerian element in Stapledon's work, especially in his future histories and most notably in *Last and First Men* (1930), his first popular success. The biological metaphor, with its images of birth, growth, maturity and decay, serves as an organizing structure and dominates this novel. Stapledon's future history adopts the Darwinian hypothesis but negates the late Victorian optimistic interpretation embodied in the idea of progress. Stapledon insists that the "tragedy of race," the eventual decay and collapse of man "must . . . be admitted in any adequate myth" (*LFM* Preface:10).

Indeed in this novel, it must be a "tragedy of race" and not of individuals. The assumptions of tragedy usually involve the requirement of choice; one cannot have a tragic hero unless the hero can somehow be said to be responsible for what happens to him or her. In *Last and First Men*, that element of free will is essentially gone. In this novel, there is *no hope for man*. To save himself, man must "awaken" and commit himself to the "spirit." But the essential qualities "to the spirit's well-being"—intelligence, honesty, truth, love, "self oblivious worship" (*LFM* 1:17)—are not possible for us. They demand "of the human brain a degree of vitality and coherence of which the nervous system of the First Men [i.e., us] was never really capable . . . the mentality of race shows signs of decline" (*LFM* 1:17). Like other species that could not adjust to their environment and were doomed, we are unable to cope with the "complexity of environment" caused by the increased mastery of physical science. Biology and temperament (which unfortunately amount to racial stereotyping) make it impossible for the First Men to overcome their "tribalism." They must die to make way for further evolution.

This perspective makes a "criticism of life"—Arnold's and Leavis's ideal—and the social function of literature utterly futile. Social criticism and the kind of satire that Stapledon writes rest on the assumption that human behavior is correctable, that it is malleable. Biological determinism denies this. Arguments for social reform that assume a biological determinism which constitutes "human nature" find themselves in hopeless contradiction. Conservatives often assume a "human nature" in their arguments against social and political reform, but it is a curious position for someone like Stapledon to be taking. Certainly, it is decidedly *un*marxian. For Marx, man does not have a nature; he has a *history*. Moreover, in the process of changing his society and nature, man changes himself. Biological determinism gives way to cultural construction. Even man's biological nature is, in part, influenced by the historical process. Somewhere Marx argues that man's five senses are the work of all history. In *Last and First Men*, Stapledon has written himself into a corner. His project for man, to create (or recreate) those spiritual values which are "based on our awareness of ourselves in relation to the universe" (McCarthy 26), is doomed from the beginning. There will be no resolution between the struggle of "two competing wills" unless we can evolve into something quite different from what we now are (McCarthy 27).

However, between *Last and First Men* and *Star Maker*, not to mention his last works, Stapledon's thinking on some of the themes raised in *Last and First Men* gains considerably in complexity and subtlety. What I wish to focus on for the rest of this essay is the way in which Stapledon attempts to resolve in *Star Maker* many of the contradictions that he dramatizes in *Last and First Men*. These contradictions are resolved in the attempt to "totalize" his vision, to "see the Whole." In one sense, it is a continuation of what I see as Stapledon's Hegelianism, but at the same time, I want to relate it to his Marxism and, finally, to discuss that move in light of structuralist and post-structuralist theory. That Stapledon adopts a "cosmic" perspective is obvious; what may not be so apparent is that as a philosopher, Stapledon was working within a long tradition going as far back as Aristotle and Plato; however, it is a tradition that has become increasingly problematic. And there is no question that Stapledon was "doing" philosophy as he wrote his fiction. As Richard Rorty has argued, if philosophy is a form of literature, then literature is a form of philosophy.

The pessimism engendered as a consequence of Stapledon's biological determinism dramatized in *Last and First Men* reaches its most extreme statement in *Odd John* (1935). John is Stapledon's vehicle for exposing the foibles of our contemporary world, and almost no institution escapes his withering gaze. Human nature is severely limited; it has reached a dead end:

> for every type of creature there's a limit of *possible* development of capacity, a limit inherent in its ground plan of organization. *Homo Sapiens* reached his limit a million years ago, but he has only recently begun to use his powers dangerously. In achieving science and mechanism he has brought about a state of affairs which cannot be dealt with properly save by a capacity which is more developed than his. (*OJ* 10:116)

Man is still subhuman; we are likened to spiders trying to crawl out of a basin (*OJ* 10:116). The bug imagery is not accidental. John is convinced that he could not remake man even if he were to try; nor does he believe an encounter with a superior alien intelligence would help us. They—the aliens—would not try to remake us but "use terrestrials as cattle or museum pieces or pets, or just vermin" (*OJ* 10:118). The reader is reminded of Swift's savage denunciation of the human race.

After such a vision, what hope? John and the other members of his group commit suicide rather than be forced to deplete their spirit by ruling our planet. They would rather die than be contaminated by us. Whether *Odd John* is an accurate reflection of Stapledon's mood at this time or not is a matter of speculation, but the message of the work itself is clear, it is the

Slough of Despond, the Everlasting Nay. If there is to be any hope for the human species, something has to be done.

There is one hope. John sees one hope for human beings: " . . . to be divinely inspired, so that their nature became truly human at a stride . . . lifted out of their pettiness by a sudden and spontaneous access of strength to their own rudimentary spiritual nature" (*OJ* 10:117). John cannot or will not do this; the superior alien will not do this. *Who* will do it? Who will assume the responsibility and take on the task? Stapledon will. He will become the source of divine inspiration. He will become Star Maker. Stapledon, the writer, will create a universe which positions the reader in such a way as to encourage him or her to receive a particular message—a message of hope.

This involves two major projects. The first task is to position the reader so that he or she in responding to the narrative will be able to overcome or at least to understand the inherent contradictions in the self, society, history, and, indeed, the whole universe. This involves writing a story which will give the reader a new perspective—what we call now Stapledon's "cosmic perspective"—a totalizing vision which will displace the various contradictions and subsume them within a historical pattern emplotted as myth—as tragedy. Once this has been done, a related project is to overcome the reader's skepticism and convince him or her that to play one part in this particular drama has been worthwhile. Stapledon attempts to do both in *Star Maker*.

I can think of no writer who has so consistently understood experience in such dualistic terms as Stapledon. *Everything* is viewed as self-contradictory, divided, polarized, etc. Leslie Fiedler's book on Stapledon is most appropriately subtitled "A Man Divided." Even the Star Maker must create twin cosmoses to embody the dual aspects of himself, one positive, creative, and aware, the other "rebellious, destructive, cynical":

> This twi-mindedness at length gave rise to a new mode of creating. There came a stage in the Star Maker's growth, as my dream represented it, when he contrived to dissociate himself as two independent spirits, the one his essential self, the spirit that sought positive creation of vital and spiritual forms and ever more lucid awareness, the other a rebellious, destructive and cynical spirit, that could have no being save as a parasite upon the works of the other. (*SM* 15:420)

These divisions operate on all levels, the psychological, social, and cosmic; or, using philosophic terminology, these contradictions permeate Stapledon's ontology, epistemology, ethics, and metaphysics.

From a structuralist perspective, one could argue that Stapledon is caught in the web of language. It is the dialectic of opposition, of difference that creates meaning. "Good" means something only in relation to "evil"; "darkness" needs light to complete itself; the "saint" is understandable only in relation to the "revolutionary"; to "awaken" has meaning only in contrast to "sleep"; we can understand our world only in contrast to other worlds;

"history" can be grasped only from the point of view of non-history (the eternal). Each term has meaning only in relation to the other term. Indeed, for someone such as the anthropologist, Levi-Strauss, the binary oppositions in language reveal the basic structure of the human mind. Contradiction *is* reality.

By the same token, these contradictions constitute Stapledon's moments of frustration, of his "undecidability," or, to put it in post-structuralist terms, of his *aporias*. Each term contains within it elements of its opposite. In the opposition between x/y, a/b, darkness/light, saint/revolutionary, etc., Stapledon is caught on the "/" of the opposition. It is a moment of impasse, a moment that has confronted philosophy from its beginning. The stasis is inherent in the project itself. It is a moment that Stapledon was not able to overcome in *Last and First Men* but attempts to do so in *Star Maker* through the cosmic perspective.

In his essay "Writers and Politics," Stapledon accepts the Marxian "account of our troubles," but he argues that the Marxist explanation is "not the whole truth." He argues that "to defend civilization we must do more than attack its enemies. We must re-affirm and clarify the civilized spirit, which is simply the developed human spirit" (153). But to do this, we must, as Stapledon says in his "Preface," be able to see "*man's life as a whole in relation to the rest of things*" (*SM* 250; emphasis mine). In short, we must see man's life in its total context; that perspective will give it meaning. The problem, of course, is that perspective means to see from a *particular* location; moreover, while meaning is context-bound, the context is boundless! Nevertheless, this attempt to grasp the totality is Stapledon's project.

Stapledon's move to overcome the binary oppositions by transcending them to grasp their "totality" is a common one in all thinking. It involves what Kenneth Burke has described as the "dialectic of the upward way." One overcomes conflict, contradiction, polar opposition by ascending to a higher level of abstraction, to a higher level of generality; one example of this would be the Hegelian dialectic of thesis/antithesis/synthesis. Ultimately, one reaches the highest level: God, or to some term that functions like God, a "god term" (in Stapledon's case, it is the Star Maker). To overcome the contradictions, to get beyond the impasse of the aporias, we must gain access to the "spirit." To do this, we must view these contradictions in relationship "to the Whole." Like Spinoza, Leibniz, and Emerson before him, Stapledon believes that if we can view man and his history from the point of view of eternity, we can better understand these contradictions and, if not overcome them, at least accept them. This is the function of the Narrator's cosmic voyage.

The strategy Stapledon adopts is a common one for intellectuals to take. In his *Marxism and Totality*, Martin Jay observes that this particular strategy is characteristic of intellectuals, who have the "time" and the "hubris to believe that they might know the whole of reality."[5] In his introduction, Jay observes that this attempt to articulate a convincing vision of totality has been one of the strongest themes in modern social thought. The term *totality* itself has positive connotations:

> The concept of totality or wholeness has generally been associated with other positively charged words, such as coherence, order, fulfillment, harmony, plenitude, meaningfulness, consensus and community. And concomitantly, it has been contrasted with such negatively valanced concepts as alienation, fragmentation, disorder, conflict, contradiction, serialization, atomization and estrangement.(21)

Jay traces this concept from classical Greek philosophy through such thinkers as Rousseau and Freud, and particularly in the thought of Western Marxism, from Georg Lukács to the Frankfurt School.

For example, Jay's discussion of Rousseau's concept of totality is very suggestive in thinking about Stapledon's notion of personality-in-community. Jay writes that "no one did more than Rousseau to dramatize the agony of personal fragmentation or searched as frantically for ways to end it." Rousseau understood "the delicate and brittle quality of the new [i.e., since the Renaissance] individualism" (40). Rousseau's solution was to propose a society in which the triumph over fragmentation was contingent on man's transcending his petty individualism and selfish desires and giving "allegiance to a higher moral community" expressed as the General Will (41).

Furthermore, Stapledon's most important metaphors for describing his totality—drama (tragedy) and music—are similar to the views of Kant (developed in *Idea of a Universal History)*, Shiller, and Schlegel, and Herbert Marcuse's vision of "aesthetic totalizations." Lukács also stressed the importance of the aesthetic in overcoming "dissonance and fragmentation" (Jay 51–52).

Of the premarxist thinkers, it is Hegel whom Stapledon most resembles. Contradiction was for Hegel—as it would be later for Marx—the "very motor of history." More important, "when the journey was completed, the contradictions and dualisms which had manifested themselves along the way would be reconciled, but the type of reconciliation achieved would also include their preservation." One consequence of Hegel's system, which is also true for Stapledon's vision, "was a theodicy in which apparent evil could be ultimately seen as part of a larger good." Another consequence "was that the journey itself was a cyclical rather than simply linear progress, for the origin, the Absolute Spirit [read Star Maker], was also the goal" (Jay 55–56).

Variations on this concept of totality—a central idea in all of Western philosophy—pervade the thinking of all of the major Marxist theoreticians in the West, from Lukács to the members of the Frankfurt School.

One Marxist thinker whom Stapledon probably never read is Ernst Bloch; however, shot through as it is with mysticism and a powerful utopian vision, Bloch's Marxism suggests uncanny parallels with Stapledon's thought. As Jay points out, "Bloch's concept of totality was all-encompassing" and was "ultimately rooted in a cosmic vision of wholeness that clearly transcended anything to be found in Marx or any of his other followers" (174). Like Stapledon, Bloch expressed his philosophy in a rich, metaphorical prose style that, while not fiction, was influenced by Expressionism. Philosophy became literature. Bloch accepted the concept of totality as articulated by other Marxist thinkers, such as Lukács, but he criticized both Hegel and Lukács for their overemphasis on the present and their neglect of the future, which Bloch saw as the difference between "appearance" and "essence," the latter distinguished by its "not-yet" quality (183). Bloch's attempt to deal with present contradictions by appealing to the future—what Jay calls a "kind of hermeneutics of prefiguration"—is strikingly similar to Stapledon's efforts in his future histories.

Moreover, Bloch insisted on "the possibility of the sudden appearance of the *Novum*, or the radically new, in the historical process, very much like the religious experience of the *Eschaton* intersecting the course of profane time" and "suggested a reliance on extra-human forces in history" (190). Influenced by the process philosophies of such men as Eduard von Hartmann and Henri Bergson, Bloch was interested in "the larger category . . . [of] the cosmic process of fulfillment, the teleological drive embodied in creative matter, of which man was only a part" (191). Not only has Bloch's thinking influenced contemporary definitions of science fiction, but his extension of the teleological into the realm of matter is suggestive of Stapledon's "conscious" stars and their cosmic dance.[6] Bloch's gnosticism, his idealistic "assumption that ideological, theoretical, or artistic expressions of hope, desire, and hunger have objective correlatives on the ontological level of the 'not yet' expressed in, but more basic than, socio-economic relations" (192), finds clear echoes in Stapledon's philosophy of "the spirit." In *Philosophy and Living* (1939), published right after *Star Maker*, Stapledon argues for the same teleological perspective which Bloch assumes:

> There seems some reason to believe that purposiveness, which in one manner or another characterises all conscious behaviour, must play a very large part in the universe . . . It is reasonable to suppose that, throughout the universe, conscious beings vary immensely both in the richness of their capacities and in the degree of integration of their capacities to form unified systems.
>
> . . . . .
>
> By means of intelligence and creative imagination conscious beings can sometimes so manipulate reality in the world and in themselves that it will manifest entirely new aspects of itself. In my earlier book, *Star Maker*, I have sketched an imaginary history of the cosmos on these lines. (*PL* II, 402, 404)

Bloch argued that "the ultimate totalization at the end of the historical process would... reconcile not merely men with themselves and their objectifications, but also men with nature, which would itself be a subject" (Jay 185). Later Marxist philosophers, such as Habermas, have criticized Bloch for ignoring social, economic, and political relations and exclusively focusing on "the sphere which Hegel reserves for Absolute Spirit" (Jay 191). One could direct the same criticism to Stapledon, to the degree that he subordinates present, historically specific, social, economic, and political problems to his cosmic perspective.

The Hegelian and Blochian elements in Stapledon's thought are revealing. There is one final comparison, however, which shows Stapledon's divergence from complete Hegelianism or Bloch's optimistic utopianism. This concerns the knowability of the Star Maker. For Hegel, "the ontological process was ultimately knowable by the human subject, whose rationality partakes of the general rationality permeating the whole... Hegel did not posit an ultimate subordination of man the maker to God the maker in terms of their relative ability to know what they had made. Man was himself a moment in the Absolute Spirit; its self-recognition was also his own" (Jay 56–57). Now, from one point of view, one would expect Stapledon to be receptive to this concept. The universe that the Star Maker makes is Stapledon's universe, and the goal of the cosmic journey is precisely to know this universe and its creator. Moreover, the cosmic voyage is not a journey outward but a journey *inward*. The medium of the Star Maker is "his own unconscious" (*SM* 15:414); it is the Narrator's "dream" that "represented" the Star Maker, and the Star Maker is Stapledon.

Yet—and perhaps this is where Stapledon is more "modern" than we would suppose—the Narrator is still teetering on the "abysses" of uncertainty (*SM* 16:430–31). In this post-Freudian world, unlike the world in which Hegel was situated, what is real is not always rational. The unconscious and dreams are not amenable to reason; the unconscious is by definition unknowable, and dreams are mysterious and must be deciphered. Hence, the Narrator concludes: "but in truth the eternal spirit was ineffable. Nothing whatever could be truly said about it" (*SM* 15:429).

"Nothing could be truly said about it" because on this cosmic journey, the Narrator and the reader encounter an endless chain of signifiers, the signifieds (the concepts) of which become other signifiers. Man is a sign to be read and understood in relation to other signs—e.g., alien worlds, various life forms, tremendous magnitudes, etc.—and to the Star Maker itself. Each world, each universe, each new spatial and temporal dimension is a signified for the preceding one—i.e., its context—and is, in turn, the signifier for the following one. Level upon level of signifiers, and the ultimate signifier, the Star Maker, is unnameable. We are again at an impasse. We are paralyzed. The ultimate vision is contemplation, not sympathy or love—"the crystal ecstasy of contemplation" (*SM* 15:429).

Recognizing that the Star Maker is ultimately unknowable and unnameable, Stapledon is facing a similar problem to the one that contemporary Marxist thinkers confront in their effort to comprehend and name their concept of totality. Ultimately, both enterprises are doomed to failure because their medium is language and, as Derrida argues, all that language can indicate is that there are " 'holes' rather than 'wholes' " (Jay 516). What Stapledon wants to do is say something about the "eternal spirit," about God or the Star Maker. However, as Cornelius Castoriadis writes, God is imaginary, and the imaginary is not identical to the symbolic. The imaginary needs the symbolic in order to be "expressed" and to "exist," but the symbolism "presupposes an imaginary capacity... the capacity to see in a thing what it is not, or see it other than it is." There is an "ultimate or radical imaginary" which functions as the "common root of the positive imaginary and symbolic" and gives the symbolic meaning (9–10). God, for Castoriadis, is an unnameable, "imaginary signification":

> He [God] is not the name or the images a people give themselves of him, nor anything similar. Conveyed and indicated by all these symbols, he is what in each religion makes these symbols into religious symbols. He is a central *signification*, one that organizes signifiers and signifieds into a system, upholds their intersecting unity, and allows their extension, multiplication, and modification. And this signification, which corresponds to neither something perceived (real) nor something thought (rational), is an imaginary signification. (23)

And just as God is an imaginary signification, so is totality, the whole, or whatever name we want to give to this all-encompassing term.

The concept of totality as it is employed in contemporary philosophy—Marxist or otherwise—has come under increasingly suspicious scrutiny, particularly in the work of the post-structuralists. If there is one theme that unites such thinkers as Jacques Derrida, Michel Foucault, Jacques Lacan, Roland Barthes, Gilles Deluze, Jean-Francois Lyotard, Julia Kristeva, and others, "it would have to be their unremitting hostility towards totality" (Jay 515). The search for totality is a quest for the holy grail of a unified, stable truth, an illusionary foundation which will unify and, hence, provide secure, unequivocal axioms upon which one can stand for the purpose of putting things in their "proper perspective." However, the post-structuralist turn in philosophy and literary theory has made the entire enterprise problematic.

That Stapledon would undertake such a quest for a totalizing cosmic vision is, of course, both understandable and, indeed, laudable. It is this cosmic vision, this totalizing perspective, that earns him the right to argue for a "tragic" view of life, to be able to say that whatever is, is right (from the point of view of eternity). While from an epistemological perspective, it may be futile to aim for a totalizing vision, it is nevertheless the case, whether we believe that this meaning is discovered or created, that we must have *meaning* in order to act at all. We need some framework within which we can make sense of life. Moreover, this is not to say that we need certainty; clearly Stapledon was beset by doubt. But we do need some vision that will give our acts meaning. Just as Kyo, the hero of Malraux's *Man's Fate*, finds "the will to dignity" in Marxism, which gives meaning to his life and death, we need positive, utopian visions. And, as Martin Jay observes, "paradoxically, even after one acknowledges all of these reasons why the discourse of totality is now so much in disfavor, it is precisely because of one of contemporary history's most frightening realities [i.e., the threat of nuclear catastrophe] that it is both impossible and unwise to abandon it entirely" (536). And that is exactly why Stapledon's works are so important today.

NOTES

1. See Fiedler, Kinnaird, and McCarthy. Satty and Smith provide the standard bibliography for Stapledon; it includes secondary sources published up to 1984.
2. See Rutledge and Swanson.
3. See Elkins.
4. However, see Tremaine's argument in "Historical Consciousness in Stapledon and Malraux."
5. See Jay, 12. Practically all of my discussion on the concept of totality has drawn heavily on Jay's excellent study.
6. See Suvin (especially chapter 4: "Science Fiction and the Novum").

WORKS CITED

Cassirer, Ernst. *Symbol, Myth, and Culture: Essays and Lectures of Ernst Cassirer 1935–45*. New Haven and London: Yale University Press, 1979.

Castoriadis, Cornelius. "The Imaginary Institution of Society." In *The Structural Allegory: Reconstructive Encounters with the New French Thought*, ed. John Fekete. [Theory and History of Literature, Volume II] Minneapolis: University of Minnesota Press, 1984.

Crossley, Robert. "Politics and the Artist: The Aesthetic of *Darkness and the Light*." *Science-Fiction Studies* 9 (November 1982): 294–305.

Eagleton, Terry. *Literary Theory: An Introduction*. Minneapolis: University of Minnesota Press, 1983.

Elkins, Charles." The Worlds of Olaf Stapledon: Myth or Fiction?" *Mosiac* 19 (Spring/Summer 1980): 145–52.

Fiedler, Leslie. *Olaf Stapledon: A Man Divided*. New York: Oxford University Press, 1983.

Jay, Martin. *Marxism and Totality: The Adventures of a Concept from Lukács to Habermas*. Berkeley and Los Angeles: University of California Press, 1984.

McCarthy, Patrick A. *Olaf Stapledon*. Boston: Twayne Publishers, 1982.

Rutledge, Amelia A. "*Star Maker*: The Agnostic Quest." *Science-Fiction Studies* 9 (November 1982): 274–83.

Ryan, Michael. *Marxism and Deconstruction: A Critical Articulation*. Baltimore and London: Johns Hopkins University Press, 1982.

Satty, Harvey J., and Curtis C. Smith. *Olaf Stapledon: A Bibliography*. Westport, Conn.: Greenwood Press, 1984.

Suvin, Darko. *The Metamorphoses of Science Fiction: On the Poetics of a Literary Genre*. New Haven and London: Yale University Press, 1979.

Swanson, Roy Arthur. "The Spiritual Factor in *Odd John and Sirius*." *Science-Fiction Studies* 9 (November 1982): 284–93.

Tremaine, Louis, "Historical Consciousness in Stapledon and Malraux." *Science-Fiction Studies* 11 (July 1984): 130–38.

5

Ritual Experience in *Odd John* and *Sirius*

Louis Tremaine

Last and First Men and *Star Maker* are indisputably central to Olaf Stapledon's unique body of work and, at the same time, are among the most formidable texts ever faced by scholars of science fiction. It is often with a mixed sense of relief and diminished expectation, therefore, that readers turn to two less demanding works, *Odd John* and *Sirius*. We can detect this sense in the tone of the critics' praise. John Kinnaird, for example, speculates that *Odd John* "may be—*simply as a novel*—Stapledon's best" (54), while Eric Rabkin, equally tentative, calls *Sirius* "perhaps Stapledon's *most readable* novel" (238; emphasis added in both cases). But these two books represent more than an occasion to reaffirm our conventional values in fiction while we solemnly admire, from a distance, the core texts. For, beyond their own separate achievements, *Odd John* and *Sirius* (and, to a lesser extent, shorter works like *A Man Divided*) develop an imaginative vision directly complementary to that of the more massive works, one which, in fact, reveals elements of Stapledon's thinking that lie otherwise buried beneath the sheer bulk of those works.

The technique by which *Last and First Men* and *Star Maker* construct their vision of the whole of human existence is one of accretion. In the former, this accretion develops through the stratification of human forms by which the Eighteenth Men eventually rise upon the foundation of all previous species. In the latter, the "disembodied, wandering view-point" (*SM* 2:268) that is the narrator gathers into himself representatives of countless other worlds, straining toward that comprehensive and eternal perspective from which the Star Maker might be glimpsed. In both books, the impact of this accretion upon an individual being (whether character or reader) takes the form of an increased ability to measure oneself relative to the larger schema, to understand the nature of one's participation in it, to see the progress of the whole of which one forms but an infinitesimal part. Such a vision, however, provides no model for individual change or progress. It is an historical vision, but one that explains and potentially shapes the transformations of collective history, not personal history.

It is precisely here that *Odd John* and *Sirius* distinguish themselves from the larger works in their attempt to trace a process of transformation in an individual life. All four books (like virtually everything Stapledon wrote) are concerned ultimately with the spiritual dimension of human existence. The difference is that that dimension is expressed in *Last and First Men* and *Star Maker* as spiritual *vision* and in *Odd John* and *Sirius* as spiritual *experience*.

The longer works, seen in this way, have as their aim to shape a vision both of the spirit that drives existence and of the potential fullness of creation's response to that spirit. This aim requires that each work balance diversities in such a way that the particular is valuable insofar as it implies the whole. The meaning of the Eleventh Men, for example, is not that they are eleventh, but that they are men, that they express certain possibilities against the background of a spectrum of all human possibilities. *Odd John* and *Sirius*, on the other hand, are not simply vision writ small, cosmic wholeness compacted into the compass of a single life. Rather they propose an *experience* of spirit and of the response to spirit that differs from vision in that the particular is selective and primary, rather than a mere element or emblem of the whole. This is not to say that the whole is unrelated to the experience of the particular—quite the contrary—but that the relationship between the two is forged afresh in a creative act of the individual, rather than worked out through some supraindividual design. Thus John seeks fulfillment in his "uniqueness" (*OJ* 3:15, 12:82) and Sirius in his "true self" (*Sirius* 7:232). Such notions figure in *Last and First Men* and *Star Maker* as well, but there "truth to self" is evaluated less by its "trueness" than by its impact on the whole—very often a negative impact, evidenced, for example, by the Fourth Men or "Great Brains" (*LFM* 11:162–66) and by the "mad worlds" (*SM* 9:352–61).

The manner in which the spiritual dimension is expressed in these works, whether as vision or as experience, determines the primary mode of activity in which the characters engage. In *Last and First Men* and *Star Maker*, where characters are most often composite beings, the characteristic mode is meditation: creating and developing a state of consciousness in which vision can flower and grow to wholeness. In *Odd John* and *Sirius*, however, where the vision of the whole gives way to the experience of the partial, the contingent, the circumstantial, and where characters are highly individual beings, it is helpful, I would suggest, to think of the primary mode of activity in which the characters engage (or, at least, to which they aspire) as ritual: perfecting and practicing a set of acts that lend spiritual consequence to lived experience.

Ritual finds its place in these works both as an event and as a condition. The more familiar understanding of ritual as an event depends largely on Arnold van Gennep's classic formulation of the structure of "rites of passage." Such rites, according to van Gennep, proceed as three-part progressions: separation (in which the subject symbolically severs his ties to his normal social and spiritual condition), transition (in which the subject performs acts, and submits himself to forces, of extraordinary symbolic power and consequence), and reincorporation (in which the subject rejoins the world of daily routine, but in an altered social and spiritual condition). The transitional, or "liminal" phase is at the center of the ritual experience. It is the moment when the subject is freed of the constraints (but also of the protections) imposed by categories and can accomplish by symbolic means what he cannot accomplish through the resources available to him in his ordinary status. Victor Turner, in his influential elaboration of van Gennep's theory, explains that

> liminal *personae* ("threshold people") are necessarily ambiguous, since . . . these persons elude or slip through the network of classifications that normally locate states and positions in cultural space. Liminal entities are neither here nor there; they are betwixt and between the positions assigned and arrayed by law, custom, convention, and ceremonial. (95)

Turner's most significant contribution to the theory of ritual, and one important for our purposes, is to develop the notion of ritual liminality beyond the level of individuals and events and to apply it as well to ongoing conditions of social relatedness:

> It is as though there are here two major "models" for human interrelatedness, juxtaposed and alternating. The first is of society as a structured, differentiated, and often hierarchical system of politico-legal-economic positions with many types of evaluation, separating men in terms of "more" or "less." The second, which emerges recognizably in the liminal period, is of society as an unstructured or rudimentarily structured and relatively undifferentiated *comitatus*, community, or even communion of equal individuals who submit together to the general authority of the ritual elders. (96)

The first of these Turner refers to as the condition of "structure" and the second as that of "communitas," terms which I intend to use in these special senses in discussing the work of Stapledon.

Several considerations by Turner make these concepts especially useful for an investigation of Stapledon's two novels. One is that, unlike van Gennep, Turner rejects as "error . . . the confusion between communitas, which is a dimension of all societies, past and present, and archaic or primitive society" (130). Indeed, Stapledon's concern is with the opposite of primitiveness. Further, this peculiarly human experience is a constitutive element of human existence, not an aberrant or extraordinary phenomenon linked to supernatural practices:

> I infer that, for individuals and groups, social life is a type of dialectical process that involves successive experience of high and low, communitas and structure, homogeneity and differentiation, equality and inequality.... In other words, each individual's life experience contains alternating exposure to structure and communitas, and to states and transitions. (97)

And finally, though it is, in Turner's terminology, a "transition" rather than a "state," communitas is a condition that is capable of being sustained over time. While the "spontaneous communitas" of ritual, narrowly understood, is highly unstable, it can sustain itself as "normative" or "ideological communitas" by entering into a relationship with structure (132), and indeed the health both of individuals and of society, in Turner's view, is dependent upon this continuing and dynamic relationship.

Turner's notion of the relationship of structure and communitas, then, provides an appropriate model by which to understand and evaluate the aims and accomplishments of the main characters in *Odd John* and *Sirius*. In applying this model, we find that these characters seek to bring a spiritual vision to bear on their immediate lives by means of ritual experience, to locate themselves within the liminal moment of ritual, and to establish lives in which the communitas engendered by ritual experience maintains itself in a certain relationship to the claims of structure. Such a model, I suggest, can help account for significant elements of the narrative technique by which these characters' actions and motivations become known to us, as well as for the defeat which eventually awaits them.

At the core of this broadly defined ritual experience, however, there is enacted by the protagonist of *Odd John* a quite conscious and intentional ritual in the strict sense, one that announces themes essential to the shape of the larger project of communitas in both books. That complex and concentrated act is John's retreat to the wilderness in chapter 12, with the killing of the stag as its centerpiece. Here we find a classic, fully elaborated initiation rite, one which exhibits precisely the stages outlined by van Gennep and Turner. It is developed, moreover, according to a particular pattern of initiation, that of ascetic ordeal. Mircea Eliade has described that pattern in terms that will be helpful to quote at length for purposes of comparison:

> The distinctive note of all these... initiations is the belief that the tutelary spirit can be won by an ascetic effort in the wilderness. The ascetic practices pursue the annihilation of the novice's secular personality, in other words, his initiatory death; in many cases, this death is announced by the ecstasy, trance, or pseudo-unconsciousness

into which he falls. Like all other intitiations, these . . . aim at the spiritual transmutation of the novice; but it is important to emphasize the cosmic context of their scenarios. The novice's solitude in the wilderness is equivalent to a *personal* discovery of the sacredness of the cosmos and of animal life. All nature is revealed as a hierophany. The passage from secular existence in the community . . . to the existence sanctified by meeting with the Gods or spirits is not made without peril. "Possessed" by the Gods or spirits, the novice is in danger of completely losing his psychomental balance. (68)

John's ascetic experience in the wilderness, it will be recalled, begins with his feeling a need to "cut right adrift" and "face the universe in absolute nakedness" (*OJ* 12:77). He seeks this state of spiritual nakedness first through physical nakedness, leaving behind not only his clothes, but all objects produced by human civilization—"separation," in van Gennep's terms. During this "terrible ordeal" he is "delirious" and literally near death (*OJ* 12:78). A kind of psychic death follows, which brings him "that unspeakable joy . . . of seeing things as it were through God's eyes, and finding them after all *right*, fitting, in the picture," and in which he rejects his former self and seeks, regardless of risk, a new birth:

I seemed to have lost touch completely with all the motives of my adventure. I just lay and wondered why I had been such a self-important fool. . . . I lashed myself into facing this spiritual decay. For even in my most abject state I vaguely *knew* that somewhere there was another "I," and a better one. Well, I set my teeth and determined to go on with the job even if it killed me. (*OJ* 12:78)

While in the ritual purity of "transition," John is discovered by others and, threatened with contamination just when he is most vulnerable, flees still deeper into the wilderness. Here he encounters the stag, with its ambiguous symbolism. "Doomed, and in the prime," it is John's double, his alter-ego with which he struggles (*OJ* 12:80). At the same time, it seems to John "to symbolize the whole normal human species," the world of structure from whose constraints John seeks to free himself (*OJ* 12:84). In facing this animal, John supplies his own ritual guidance by a strong and repeated act of imagination:

"It was as though all the hunters of the past challenged me," he said, "and as though . . . the angels of God ordered me to do this little mighty deed in preparation for mightier deeds to come." (*OJ* 12:80)

The hunters of all the ages saluted him, for he had done what none of them could have done. A child, he had gone naked into the wilderness and conquered it. And the angels of heaven smiled at him, and beckoned him to a higher adventure. (*OJ* 12:81)

The nature and importance of that more mature calling become clearer to him: "the things I could *do*, the *beauty* I could make, and the *worship* that I was now beginning to conceive . . . *must* be brought to fruition" (*OJ* 12:83). Having accomplished the initiatory task set him, he then returns to civilization, celebrating his new powers through the "miracle" he performs for McWhist and Norton and translating his new knowledge into terms the uninitiated Fido can grasp. "Reincorporated" at last into the life of the world, but as a new being, he has "acquired that indefinable peacefulness and strength which is quite impossible to the adolescent of the normal species, and is very seldom acquired even by the mature," and is now ready to take up "the life of the spirit" (*OJ* 12:85).

In Eliade's language, then, John has won his tutelary spirit (the ancient hunters and angels figured in his imagination) by an ascetic effort in the wilderness. His initiatory death, announced by various threats to his psycho-mental balance (delirium), has prepared his spiritual transmutation, his personal discovery of the cosmos and of animal life (including the stag as well as *Homo sapiens*), and his passage from a secular to a sanctified existence. At the center of this extended initiatory rite, moreover, there is embedded a further ritual pattern, that of sacrifice. It is in the sacrificial aspect of the ritual that the function of the stag as John's double becomes important. For in those cultures in which blood sacrifice is practiced, as J. H. M. Beattie explains, the victim "stands for . . . the person or persons who are making the sacrifice or upon whose behalf the sacrifice is being made" (30). Henri Hubert and Marcel Mauss, to whom most modern anthropological work on sacrifice is indebted, analyze this substitution as a communication of the profane with the sacred through an intermediary:

> If the religious forces are the very principle of the forces of life, they are in themselves of such a nature that contact with them is a fearful thing for the ordinary man. . . . If he involved himself in the rite to the very end, he would find death, not life. The victim takes his place. It alone penetrates into the perilous domain of sacrifice. (98)

John is, of course, no "ordinary man," and *will* involve himself in the rite to the very end and find death. For the present, however, that end is to be deferred. According to Beattie, "almost always sacrifice is seen as being, mostly, about *power*, or *powers*" (37), and this particular sacrifice is mostly about John's own powers. Tested and expended on the stag in an ambiguous act that partakes both of worshipful praise and violence, those ambivalent powers unfold their creative potential without destroying him who generates them. The stag is indeed a "symbol," as Fido repeatedly calls it, but, for John, an efficacious one. As the central symbol of a ritual sacrifice, it both articulates John's intention and channels power in a direction consistent with that intention.

In all of these respects, then, John's initiation conforms closely to a general model as well as to particular patterns familiar to those who study ritual practice and belief. Where Stapledon significantly modifies this model and these patterns is in the amplitude of the transitional or liminal stage of the ritual. John devotes himself, over a period of months, to several extended and overlapping pursuits: the physical furbishing of his retreat through a transformation of the stag into food, clothing, and tools; various forms of aesthetic development; and a spiritual discipline ranging from contemplation to telepathic exploration to what he is content to let Fido think of as self-hypnosis. No mere symbolic passage from one state to another, this is a whole existence in microcosm. In it are contained all the elements of physical inventiveness, artistic experimentation, and spiritual advancement that are to characterize his life to come. All that is missing are those other beings who will share John's communitas with him—and it is at this time, in fact, that John first begins to stretch out his mind toward those beings: "in a telepathic way I had begun to get something very like evidence that after all I was not the only one of my kind in the world, that there were in fact quite a number of us scattered about in different countries" (*OJ* 12:84). Neither a "primitive" event nor a momentary retreat from the business of living, then, John's adventure in the wilderness becomes, for him, constitutive of the human project at its highest and a figure for ritual experience sustained in ordinary time and space.

This episode, I have suggested, can help to guide our understanding of the manner in which the protagonist pursues that project and engages in that experience, both in *Odd John* and in *Sirius*. Of particular importance in this respect is the dialectic it develops between the animal and the spiritual, a dialectic reconciled within John as a liminal being. Animal imagery is, in fact, common throughout both *Odd John* and *Sirius*. It is easy to read this in the conventional way, as designating that which is subhuman and loathsome. John often refers to normal human beings disparagingly as animals and expresses his "revulsion and horror" at Europa's caresses by comparing her to a dog, a monkey, and a donkey (*OJ* 8:52). Sirius's biographer describes a distressing conflict between "his 'wolf-nature' and his compassionate civilized mentality" (*Sirius* 3:181). But John's stag, it must be remembered, is a creature of "beauty and freedom" which John "knew... and praised" (*OJ* 12:79, 82). Nor, as it turns out, is this animal an exception, but an emblem for something highly valued in nature, in humanity, and in John himself. This value is what John calls "style," something he finds, for example, in

> studying the sea-birds, for which he had a surprising passion. This interest, which at times seemed almost obsessive, he explained... by saying, "They do their simple jobs with so much more *style* than man shows in his complicated job." (*OJ* 5:27)

He responds to the same value in his friend Judy, explaining her importance to him succinctly, if ungrammatically: "I'm fond of Judy as I'm fond of sea-birds. She does only simple things, but she does them all with style. She be's Judy as thoroughly and perfectly as a gannet be's a gannet" (*OJ* 6:35). The fishermen Abe and Mark, too, he praises as "damned fine stuff" for sticking to what they can do and doing it well, unlike most of ordinary humanity (*OJ* 9:56). To "be" himself, then, to find *his own* style (*OJ* 6:35), and by being himself to take his place as an animal in nature, is a part of what John is called to in the wilderness.

In *Sirius*, the situation would seem to be the reverse: if John is a spiritual being reaching down to the animal in himself and in his world, Sirius is an animal straining upward to become spirit. But the relationship between these two halves of his nature is more complicated, as we see in his discovery of himself as animal: "Hunting now gripped Sirius as the main joy of life; but it was a guilty joy. He felt its call almost as a religious claim upon him, the claim of the dark blood-god for sacrifice" (*Sirius* 3:181). Even in his puppyhood, Sirius begins to think of his "wolf-nature" not simply as inhuman instinct, but as a response to something god-like, however "dark." As he grows, he develops in extraordinary ways not only spiritually, but as an animal, training himself to survive splendidly on the moor and cultivating those senses that are particular to him as a dog. Sirius may, then, be thought of as an inversion of John, not because, as a super-dog, he is as far below the human as the superhuman John is above it, but because the "animal" in Sirius is a "dark" version of the "spirit" in John. It is, in fact, the higher mode for Sirius, turning "dark" only when it is in conflict with the rule-bound, structured world of human civilization. Sirius is indeed reaching from his animal self toward a spirit self, but in so doing he is reaching from strength to strength.

That spirit self lies persistently beyond his individual reach, however, forcing him to seek the desired reconciliation through association with other beings. The claim is made several times that such associations come naturally to Sirius as a dog, that "dogs excelled in social awareness" (*Sirius* 2:172). That claim is not supported, however, by example. In *Sirius*, dogs pursue their social life by fighting, copulating, and serving man together—they do not form spiritual communities. Sirius, in fact, is content to see his own offspring drowned or sold off (*Sirius* 12:272). He cannot, of course, look to others of his own particular kind, for they do not exist. It is to humanity, therefore, that he turns for the needed counterpart. Such an alliance presents itself to him imaginatively in a vision of what he calls (echoing the narrator of *Star Maker*) "the supreme moment." This vision is couched in terms of fragrances and the hunt, terms proper to his animal nature, and the imagined reconciliation affirms that nature, as Sirius sees himself led "to the universal Master, the superhuman master whom my super-canine nature so desperately needed to take possession of me and steady me with his claim for absolute loyalty and service." Though this vision is only an imaginative event, Sirius concludes from it "that it does indeed matter to be as quickened a spirit as possible, and to live for the quickening of the spirit everywhere," that he is "going to be the hound of the spirit" (*Sirius* 9:248).

Both John and Sirius, then, discover their animal selves in the wilderness, but to incorporate those essential selves into a sustainable spiritual existence they must leave the wilderness and seek community. The relationships into which they enter largely correspond to what Stapledon describes in *Philosophy and Living* as "personality-in-community" and in *Saints and Revolutionaries* as "individuality-in-community" (both published in 1939, midway between *Odd John* and *Sirius*). Such a relationship, for Stapledon, is not marginal or aberrant, but a direct expression of "an essential underlying kinship and identity in all possible kinds of conscious being" (*PL* 403). "Kinship and identity," however, are not to be understood as sameness. Significant spiritual community, in fact, requires an amalgam of singly directed but diverse beings of diverse experience:

> The whole gamut of these experiences contributes to our awareness of community. ...But the kind of relationship which is most significant, and the norm of all the others, is that in which each individual is clearly aware of himself and of the other; and in which the two are of very diverse character, bound in mutual respect and mutual enrichment, and in a common task. (*SR* 140)

What makes the normal species normal, in *Odd John*, is not simply its limited intelligence, but precisely its inability to achieve such individuality-in-community. By the same token, what makes John's colony "super-normal" is not simply the intelligence of its members, but more significantly its capacity for community *based upon* (and not merely in the face of) extreme diversity. Indeed, in focusing on the distinctions between the super-normals and ordinary human beings, the reader may fail to notice just how diverse a crowd this is that John has brought together. Despite the narrator's speculation about a common genetic origin somewhere in central Asia, Stapledon is careful to scatter these characters all over the globe, endowing them with widely differing physical appearances, personalities, and personal and cultural experiences. When John says, near the end, "we are one together now, and there is no life for us apart" (*OJ* 21:148), this oneness refers not to a common likeness, but to a common commitment. That commitment is to "the true life of the spirit," what he understood at the completion of his initiation but could not, on his own, achieve: "It's doing everything that comes along to be done, and doing it not only with all one's might but with—spiritual taste, discrimination, *full* consciousness of what one is doing" (*OJ* 12:86). It is the spiritual concomitant to the animal virtue of "style," a rightness of gesture that transcends the rule and habit of ordinary existence and accedes to the symbolic status of ritual.

Sirius, whose publication followed that of *Philosophy and Living* and *Saints and Revolutionaries*, casts the relationship of Sirius to his possible communities in language that more closely resembles that of the philosophical works: "strange indeed was his relation to Plaxy! So alien were they in native propensity, yet so united in common history and in essential spirit" (*Sirius*

7:225); "he also, in his own incomparable creations [according to a fantasy of his], expressed the fundamental identity-in-diversity of all spirits" (*Sirius* 9:245). And yet the individual-in-community concept is a much more problematic one here than it is in *Odd John*. Sirius comes earlier than John to an understanding of his spiritual need to join individual and community, but regards the possibility of fulfilling that need more skeptically. In his music, for example, the distance between the two seems insuperable: "Either he must express himself with full sincerity but in utter loneliness, unappreciated by dogs or men; or, for the sake of his underlying brotherhood with man, he must violate his finer canine sensibility" (*Sirius* 6:218). While "the old family life" of the Trelone household affords "to every member the invaluable experience of belonging to a true community" (*Sirius* 6:213), it is not a spiritual community and does not long satisfy him. The very possibility of such a community among human beings seems to him tenuous at best:

> Just now and then they seemed somehow to create or to be gathered up into something lovelier than their individual selves, something which demanded their selves' sacrifice and yet gave their selves new life. But how precariously, torturingly; and only just for a flicker of time! (*Sirius* 8:244)

It is only in Plaxy that he finds a spiritual longing to correspond to his own. In their love, he finds "at heart a religious love for the universal spirit" (*Sirius* 10:256), "a bright gem of community" (*Sirius* 12:268), and yet there is an instability, as well, even at the heart of the relationship:

> It was . . . with Plaxy that he had found the essence of love, the close mutual dependence and sharing. Yet strangely it was often the thought of Plaxy that wakened the other mood in him, in which he rebelled against humanity's dominance. (*Sirius* 7:224)

To the super-normals' island colony, then, corresponds Sirius-Plaxy in their cottage at Tan-y-Voel. Each community is conscious, from the outset, that its duration will be limited and each sets itself a spiritual task, though the directions of their efforts are strikingly different. For the colony, the task is an outwardly directed one: "they must apprehend existence as precisely and zestfully as they could, and salute That in the universe which was of supreme excellence," offering "to the universal Spirit . . . a bright and peculiar jewel of worship" (*Sirius* 12:144–45). For Sirius-Plaxy, the goal is simply to subsist: "perhaps it will not last long, but it is real while it lasts. And there is a rightness in it. It had to be, to make us one in spirit for ever, whatever else may come" (*Sirius* 14:289). The two communities are constituted, however, in a fundamentally similar manner. Each takes that which is symbolically present in the privileged time and space of ritual—the union of nature and cosmos, of animal and spirit, of physical and mystical—and attempts to actualize and sustain it in ordinary time and space. For the spontaneous communitas that binds together ritual co-participants, as Turner has it, is substituted the normative communitas that generates its own rudimentary and specialized structure while obliterating the material categories and distinctions of full-blown and conventional structure, as manifested in normal social institutions.

It is the protagonist's experience of normal social institutions, in fact, that leads directly, in both books, to the pivotal experience (John's initiation, Sirius's vision) that in turn produces a recognition of the goal of communitas. Both characters conduct purposeful "research" that brings them into contact with a range of human activities. For John, this research is a carefully planned series of interviews conducted with business magnates, cabinet ministers, psychiatrists, priests, communists—the whole array of "individuals and types, institutions and movements" which are reported on in chapters 9 and 10 (*OJ* 10:58). For Sirius, it is the plan to "be 'shown round a bit' by Elizabeth, . . . meeting her friends in Cambridge and elsewhere," doing "a bit of sight-seeing, if it could be arranged—slums, factories, docks, museums, concerts" (*Sirius* 7:233). Both characters encounter these institutions in directly functional ways as well, through John's money-making activities and Sirius's work with Thomas's colleagues at Cambridge. These experiences are a descent into structure, from which each character emerges newly determined to live otherwise. For John, structure manifests itself as a compartmentalizing intelligence that blocks any integrated understanding of experience: "Your trouble, as a species, is that you can't keep hold of everything at once. Any one who is very wide awake toward one set of facts invariably loses sight of all the other equally important sets" (*OJ* 10:64). He concludes that he must "begin with . . . interior discovery of objective reality, in preparation for objective creation," (*OJ* 10:70), announces, "I'm through with your bloody awful species" (*OJ* 10:72), and disappears into the wilderness. Sirius's research teaches him that the world of structure consigns individuals to conventionalized roles in which their devotion to the whole is distorted by "their inveterate self-love" and "their self-deception" (*Sirius* 8:243). This discovery brings upon him the "wolf-mood" and self-admonition: "Get on with it! You have unique powers . . . and you exist to make your contribution to the world. Find your calling" (*Sirius* 9:245). These in turn lead directly to his vision of the "supreme moment" and to "a firm resolution about his future": to return to the moor—"Somehow in that world he must express whatever potency it was that was always straining in him to find exercise" (*Sirius* 10:256–57).

Both characters, then, reject the paralyzing categories and conventions of structure and are eventually drawn instead to the internally boundless world of communitas, of sustained liminality, instinctively at first, and later by a consciously articulated effort. A sign of this orientation is the degree to which their acts reveal not only a practical but a ritual impulse. That impulse, as we have seen, is an ambiguous one, and that ambiguity, as often as not, expresses itself in moral terms. In so doing, it alienates many of Stapledon's readers.

Odd John, with its burglaries, incest, murders, and human experimentation, seems especially troubling in this respect, though the murders of humans and animals and the bestiality in *Sirius* tend to discomfit readers as well. Leslie Fiedler, for example, characterizes *Odd John* as sado-masochistic pornography (118), while John Kinnaird, in a more thoughtful analysis, sees in Smithson's murder "our first indication that John . . . is blind to the true source and end of 'spirit' . . . in the sanctity of the personality" (57). And Roy Arthur Swanson cautions that

> however important it may be to recognize the prudery of narrow-mindedness and of conventional morality, we cannot brush aside the profound moral ramifications of the murder of a member of one's own species and of copulation with a member of a different species in the interest of special mutation. (289)

In Patrick A. McCarthy's discussion of *Odd John*, however, we begin to get at the significance of these problematic elements:

> Two incidents—the murder of a policeman and the slaying of a stag—will illustrate the nature of the spiritual crisis that John faces and the pattern of his spiritual development. Both events derive ultimately from John's estrangement from the rest of mankind and his search for his own identity apart from the norms of human society. (58)

In linking Smithson and the stag and in describing John as purposefully acting outside of societal norms, McCarthy is directing our attention to a more complex view that includes not only the very real moral repugnance of John's actions, but their significance for the larger shape of his spiritual experience.

An understanding of John's and Sirius's lives as ritually conditioned helps us to see that what is involved here is not merely a negative "estrangement," but a positive reordering of experience. We have already seen the ritual elements in the killing of the stag and have seen that it is an ambivalent event. John makes it clear that he considers the stag a magnificent creature with every right to live undisturbed and, upon its death, "he burst[s] into spontaneous tears." And yet he claims that the stag's "death was [its] life's crown" (*OJ* 12:81–82). The sacrifice, then, is no mere gesture, but an act of grave moral consequence—and the consequences of the act are morally ambiguous. This moral ambiguity, furthermore, is not incidental to this particular act, but is a constitutive feature of all sacrifice in which an "innocent" victim is, as we have seen, substituted for the beneficiary of the sacrifice. The killing of Smithson, though more spontaneous, conforms to this pattern. John considers the possibility that he could kill himself instead of Smithson, but concludes that "the killing just [has] to be" (*OJ* 5:32–33). The force of this hesitation is not to convince the reader of John's moral sensitivity and thereby excuse his crime (which it has understandably failed to do with most critics), but to emphasize the function of Smithson as a sacrificial substitute for John. And it is an efficacious substitution: not only in practical terms—John survives and escapes arrest—but in symbolic ones as well, altering his spiritual status—"in that time," he says, "I saw myself and my world as never before" (*OJ* 5:32). Similarly, in *Sirius*, the killing of Thwaites is consciously given symbolic import:

> In this symbolic act he would kill not only Thwaites but the whole tyrant race. Henceforth all beasts and birds should live naturally, and the planet's natural order should never again be disturbed by the machinations of this upstart species. (*Sirius* 11:264)

The "sudden freakish impulse" that leads Sirius to kiss "the forehead of his slaughtered brother" (*Sirius* 11:265) is, again, not a bid for moral sympathy, but an affirmation of Thwaites' intended sacrificial role.

This moral ambiguity, moreover, is essential not only to sacrifice, but to the ritual moment in general. Anthropological literature abounds in reports of violations and inversions of normal laws and taboos within the special confines of ritual—stealing, sexual intercourse with normally forbidden partners, disrespectful treatment of superiors and elders, etc. The function of such practices is to free the subject from the constraints of structure so that he can reconstitute himself as a new social or spiritual being. And so it is in *Odd John* and *Sirius*. The attacks upon Stephen and Diawl Du, the dubious sexual relations with Pax and Plaxy, the killing of the crew of the Frome and of various domestic animals, and other acts of the sort are all violations of social norms—breaking of taboo, as Fido characterizes one such incident (*OJ* 8:53)—whose consequences are not only (sometimes not at all) practical, but explicitly symbolic. Those readings which condemn these acts as morally outrageous, then, distort their significance. It would be equally distorting, however, to accept them as morally justified or without moral consequence. What is needed, rather, is to see these acts as morally ambiguous and to understand that ambiguity to be constitutive and irreducible. Such ambiguity is a fundamental element of the tension between structure and communitas and that tension, we have seen, is what is centrally problematic for the protagonists of these novels.

At least partial responsibility for the moral problems these novels present, as Fiedler and Swanson correctly observe, lies with the narrators. Indeed, it is the manner of narration that sustains not only the moral ambiguity we have just seen, but the entire relationship between the liminal experience of the characters and the structural perspective of the implied reader.

All narrators are, by definition, intermediaries, but Stapledon's narrators, in these works as in all of his most significant fiction, are intermediaries in an especially strong sense. Neither omniscient, authorial narrators nor principals recounting their own stories, Fido and Robert are onlookers, feet firmly planted in normal social reality, involved in the events they record either peripherally or not at all. They are (with certain exceptions, to be discussed) so far removed from the actual experiences they report, in fact, that they occasionally go out of their way to account for their sources: letters, subsequent conversations, and the like (e.g., *OJ* 18:118; *Sirius* 1:169). They offer "theories" about these experiences rather than explanations (e.g., *OJ* 3:18; *Sirius* 14:289). And they make it clear that there are strict limits to the reliability of these reports and theories. Robert, for example, warns us that he is a novelist and will use his imagination to flesh out the story of Sirius where his information is thin, though he claims that "with imagination and self-criticism one can often penetrate into the essential spirit of events even when the data are superficial" (*Sirius* 1:169). Fido declares himself at the outset to be "a very incompetent biographer" (*OJ* 1:6) and often reaffirms this incompetence in the face of events that matter crucially to the story: "it is obviously quite impossible for me to give anything like a true account of the spiritual side of John's adventure in the wilderness" (*OJ* 12:81–82). But he too equivocates about the value of his distortions: "even if as a matter of fact I have merely misunderstood what he told me, my misunderstanding afforded at least to me a real enlightenment" (*OJ* 12:82). The narrators of *Last and First Men* and *Star Maker*, too, are "docile but scarcely adequate" (*LFM* 13) recorders who nevertheless distinguish factual from spiritual truth:

> Yet, however false the vision in detail of structure, even perhaps in its whole form, in temper surely it was relevant; in temper perhaps it was even true. The real itself, surely, had impelled me to conceive that image, false in every theme and facet, yet in spirit true. (*SM* 16:430)

Their function as intermediaries, therefore, is not merely to report, but to translate. The reader is not brought into the vision—is, in fact, explicitly excluded from it. Rather, a "poetic" or "mythic" account is set before the reader and said to "stand for" the vision, which remains a "dread mystery" (*SM* 16:430), protected from the direct gaze of those not authentically initiated into that mystery. The function of the mediating narrators in *Odd John* and *Sirius* is precisely the same. They report to the reader that something wonderful has happened and describe it in terms that can be understood by the uninitiated, but maintain a protective distance between the reader's world of structure and the actual experience of liminality by presenting an account that only "stands for" that experience.

The narrative technique in both these works, then, furthers the development of an understanding of the protagonists' experience as ritual in nature. There are, though, some important differences in the degree to which Stapledon commits himself to this mediating role of the narrator in each book. It will be useful, in this respect, therefore, to take up each text separately. As we turn first to *Odd John*, it is helpful to recall Curtis C. Smith's observation that "*Odd John* is completely different from most other superman stories, in which the concentration is usually on the drama of discovery" (54). The narration is indeed remarkable for its lack of suspense, of a sense of "story." Fido quotes John, for example, on the subject of burglary in a way that completely undercuts the potential suspense of the murder to which his burglaries lead him: "I first set about studying the technique, partly by reading, partly by discussing the subject with my friend the policeman whom I was afterwards forced to kill" (*OJ* 5:31). In the first extended paragraph of the novel, in fact, Fido recounts "the amazing facts of [John's] career" and promises, "I shall tell the world all that I can remember" (*OJ* 1:5). At the same time, he admits, "I knew almost nothing of the inner, the real John," thus announcing what is to be of central concern in this account—not events, but experience. Events are relevant not for their anecdotal outcome, but for their symbolic correspondance to an experience of meaning that lies beyond the world in which incidents combine into structured plots according to rules of plausibility. Increasingly these events are of a nature to defy such combination. Incidents of telepathy, time travel, psychic control of matter, voluntary manipulation of autonomic functions, and the like, all help to establish the fluidity, the freedom from structure and boundaries, that characterizes the ritual moment and that the super-normals intend to sustain in the ongoing liminality of communitas. Increasingly these characters observe a rule of silence, communicating in a language of gesture, image, and shared vision. Fido—not necessarily by choice, but because of what he is—observes that rule of silence regarding the details of the super-normals' mysteries. He confesses apologetically, "I have reached the part of my narrative that I intended to present with most detail and greatest effect, but several attempts to tackle it have finally convinced me that the task is beyond my powers" (*OJ* 20:134). He tells us all that he can—and all that is important—not *how* these "miracles" come about, but *that* they do. The narrator is partially responsible, therefore, not only for the moral ambiguity of his subject for the reader, but for its ambiguity at *every level* at which it comes into contact with the normal social and intellectual order.

The importance of Stapledon's treatment of ambiguity here can be better appreciated if we compare it to his handling of similar ambiguities in his philosophical writing. In *Philosophy and Living*, for example, he proposes a "theory of mystical experience" which, he acknowledges, raises "a very serious difficulty. How can the mystical attitude of delighted acceptance of the universe as perfect be reconciled with the moral attitude which . . . recognises an obligation to struggle for the good against the bad . . . ?" Much like some of his own critics, he finds the stance of the mystic "dangerous because it may lead to a complacent acquiescence in the misfortunes of others, as being 'all in the picture,' all needed for the perfection of the universe" (*PL* 425). His tentative "solution" is as follows:

> We may regard the human mind as having two aspects. In the one aspect a man is a finite individual; and his concern, his whole duty, is to champion the cause of personality-in-community in the human world. . . .

> Let us suppose, however, that he has also another aspect, in which... he recognizes intuitively that... all the struggle and defeat and agony of finite minds, no less than their partial triumph, are justified by the perfection of the whole....
>
> ...[F]or the wise conduct of practical life both are needed. (*PL* 426–27)

Here, in essence, Stapledon attempts to reconcile two opposing "attitudes" by simply calling them "aspects" instead. As a logical proposition, this is highly unsatisfying. In a work of imaginative literature, however, where resolutions are aesthetic rather than rhetorical, and where suspension of disbelief is a natural function of the reader rather than an arbitrary and awkward mental operation, it is possible to pose a problem and yet refuse all solution, embracing instead ambiguity as the higher truth. Such is the accomplishment of Stapledon's narrator in *Odd John*.

In *Sirius*, the narrator shares Fido's role as intermediary between liminal experience and structural understanding, as we have seen, but he hesitates between these two strategies (aesthetic and rhetorical) for handling ambiguity. Before retreating to his role of observer and recorder (a function embraced immediately by Fido), Robert first thrusts himself forward as a major player: "Plaxy and I had been lovers" (*Sirius* 1:165). Then he introduces a mystery: Plaxy has suddenly disappeared, but has begun to write puzzling and disturbing letters. He tracks her down, gathering evidence of still greater mystery along the way. Then he hears an "articulate but inhuman" voice, then sees Plaxy and a dog, with the attention all given to Plaxy, and *only then*, in the ninth paragraph of the book, does Robert say, "for the first time I took note of this remarkable creature," Sirius (*Sirius* 1:166). Conflict soon arises and plans are made to resolve it—but, Robert cryptically remarks, "a different fate lay in store for us" (*Sirius* 1:169). Robert the character soon recedes, however, along with all this highly conventional apparatus of suspense, to be replaced by a narrator whose own persona, far more even than Fido's, is virtually absent from most of the account.

What then ensues narratively is essentially similar to what we find in *Odd John*, with one significant difference: a persistent note of irony. Though John often speaks of his own projects and ideas ironically—and, indeed, is acutely aware of the irony at the heart of his very existence—Fido never permits himself an ironic voice in speaking of John. Robert, however, reports Sirius's reflections on canine social sensitivity, for example, in the following language:

> It was all due to man's horrible selfishness, *he told himself*.... Even dogs, of course, were self-centred, but also far more spontaneously social.... They were much more ready to be loyal absolutely, without any secret nosing after self-advantage. *So he told himself*. (*Sirius* 8:242–43; emphasis added).

Sirius's dreams of musical accomplishment he calls "grandiose fantasies," and his vision of the "supreme moment" he characterizes as "turgid stuff, but significant of his unwholesome state" (*Sirius* 9:245–46). What passes for genuine wisdom and spiritual insight in *Odd John*, then, is often reduced to naiveté in *Sirius*. This gently but unmistakably ironic stance taken by the narrator toward Sirius drops away only in the final two chapters, where Robert himself becomes part of the community of Sirius-Plaxy at Tan-y-Voel. Recognizing that this development contradicts the latent competition between himself and Sirius, he accounts for it in terms that are purely rhetorical:

> But little by little the identical spirit in each of us, as Sirius himself said, triumphed over the diversity of our natures and our private interests. Had I not actually experienced this close-knit triple relationship I should not have believed it possible. (*Sirius* 16:298)

And, indeed, we who have neither "actually experienced" it nor seen it developed narratively do *not* believe it possible. Robert abandons his role as intermediary here and assimilates himself to the experience he has been observing, but does so without taking part in the spiritual vision to which that experience corresponds for Sirius and Plaxy, as if the experience were available without the vision, without the long journey from structure into liminality that Sirius and Plaxy have undertaken. Art, however, refuses such a development and consigns it to rhetoric. Taken together, then, this narrative pattern suggests that, in the nine years since the composition of *Odd John* and seven since *Star Maker* (including the opening years of World War II), Stapledon's confidence in the power of art to sustain ambiguity in creative tension is not in *Sirius* what it had been in *Odd John*.

What this difference in turn points to is the extent to which both of these images of experience are dependent upon artistic will to maintain them erect. For, while both accounts present the experience of the protagonist as a composite of significant elements of ritual, there are significant elements *absent* as well, elements that the narrative intermediary must either supply speculatively or do without. One of these elements is sacred history. Both John and Sirius, we have seen, are seeking to attain to that continuing state of ritual experience that I have called, after Turner, communitas. But traditionally, according to Eliade, the initiation by which such a passage is brought about

> is equivalent to introducing the novice to the mythical history of the tribe; in other words, the initiand learns the deeds of the Supernatural Beings, who, in the dream times, established the present human condition and all the religious, social, and cultural institutions of the tribe. (39)

Further, for Turner, the ritual community established upon this history is limited to those "who submit together to the general authority of the ritual elders" (96). For John and Sirius, however, there is no history and the elders, who either are not there or are ignored, are a second significant element missing from their search for communitas. The "tutelary spirits" that John imagines in the wilderness, the ancient hunters and angels, are indeed imaginary and do not represent actual guidance. John instead reinvents initiation by ascetic ordeal as ontogeny recapitulates phylogeny, not as cultures intentionally reproduce themselves. In the process, he discovers his own powers, uses those powers to learn that there are others like him in the world, and conceives the project of living "the true life of the spirit." All of this, however, proceeds from within him. What the spirit *is*, what *its* powers are, and how John or any of us came to be creatures of the spirit are parts of a story that lies beyond the reach of John's solipsistic initiation. The existence of such a story is implicit—and at the end there is entrusted to Fido "an amazing document, written by John himself, and purporting to give an account of the whole story of the Cosmos" (*OJ* 22:154), an apparent anticipation of *Star Maker*. This account does not, however, emerge to organize John's identity or to explain the instinctive calling he feels. John does seek out ritual elders—Adlan, Jacqueline, and Langatse—but all three decline to be part of John's colony, offering advice only from afar. The colony is to be essentially an affair of children, as all but one of the colonists are younger than John. The three elders have embedded themselves in culture—*human* culture, regardless of distinctions between normal and super-normal—and conducted their spiritual exercises from there. John has refused that embeddedness and made a radical choice of communitas over structure. But, as we have seen, Turner's analysis points to a dialectic that excludes such radical choices:

> Wisdom is always to find the appropriate relationship between structure and communitas under the *given* circumstances of time and place, to accept each modality when it is paramount without rejecting the other, and not to cling to one when its present impetus is spent. (139)

In cutting himself off from culture, and in the absence of the explanatory power of sacred history, the present impetus is the only impetus John has. That the world of structure comes crashing in on him at the end, then, is not simply the tragic end of a noble experiment, but has more specific significance as a function of the inherent instability of ritual experience utterly disengaged from the world of structure that surrounds it.

In *Sirius*, Stapledon plays out the same drama, but eliminates the protagonist's option to seek a balance in this dialectic of structure and communitas. Sirius is truly the only one like himself. The creation story, for him, has a laboratory for its setting and a human scientist in the role of progenitor. He is excluded from human culture, dependent upon himself for every advance, and limited, for community, to a single other being who, like him, is "not quite human" (*Sirius* 4:198). In *Odd John*, the characters whose experience is the subject of the book break under the strain, leaving only an ambiguous narrative intact. In *Sirius*, the narrative itself collapses.

We began by observing that Stapledon's spiritual biographies supply what is implicit but undeveloped in the cosmic histories, complementing vision with experience. What we can now see is that the relationship between the two sets of works is reciprocal. For in those histories is the missing cultural framework needed to give visionary shape, in the biographies, to ritual experience.

WORKS CITED

Beattie, J. H. M. "On Understanding Sacrifice." In *Sacrifice*, ed. M. F. C. Bourdillon and Meyer Fortes. London: Academic Press, 1980.

Eliade, Mircea. *Rites and Symbols of Initiation: The Mysteries of Birth and Rebirth*. Trans. Willard R. Trask. New York: Harper and Row, 1958.

Fiedler, Leslie A. *Olaf Stapledon: A Man Divided*. Oxford: Oxford University Press, 1983.

Hubert, Henri, and Marcel Mauss. *Sacrifice: Its Nature and Function*. Trans. W. D. Halls. Chicago: University of Chicago Press, 1964.

Kinnaird, John. *Olaf Stapledon*. [Starmont Reader's Guide, 21] Mercer Island, Wash.: Starmont House, 1986.

McCarthy, Patrick A. *Olaf Stapledon*. Boston: Twayne Publishers, 1982.

Rabkin, Eric. "The Composite Fiction of Olaf Stapledon." *Science-Fiction Studies* 9 (November 1982): 238–48.

Smith, Curtis C. "Olaf Stapledon's Dispassionate Objectivity." In *Voices for the Future*, ed. Thomas D. Clareson. Bowling Green, Ohio: Bowling Green University Popular Press, 1976.

Swanson, Roy Arthur. "The Spiritual Factor in *Odd John* and *Sirius*." *Science-Fiction Studies* 9 (November 1982): 284–93.

Turner, Victor, W. *The Ritual Process*. Chicago: Aldine, 1969.

Van Gennep, Arnold. *The Rites of Passage*. Trans. Monika B. Vizadour and Gabrielle L. Caffee. Chicago: University of Chicago Press, 1960.

6

Diabolical Intelligence and (Approximately) Divine Innocence

Curtis C. Smith

Of those who know Olaf Stapledon today, most know his fiction. For every reader of *A Modern Theory of Ethics*, probably a hundred have read *Last and First Men*. But if Stapledon the writer of speculative fiction is more familiar than Stapledon the philosopher, Stapledon the public man, the writer of letters to the editor, the backer of political causes, is more obscure still. It is about this third Stapledon, the activist, that I shall speak in this paper. And I shall argue that one cannot fully understand the first Stapledon without understanding the third.

I shall discuss the struggles of the public Stapledon between 1935 and 1940, with particular reference to a long exchange of letters with one "Ignotus" in the pages of the *Liverpool Daily Post* (LDP). Seen from one perspective, one must conclude that Stapledon's end of this extensive correspondence is inadequate, at times woefully so, not only as a response to Ignotus but to the gathering storm in general. One must, of course, be careful not to overgeneralize from newspaper contributions, brief and overedited as they are; and one must not ask too much of a pacifist position in the late 1930s. But I shall examine Stapledon's inadequate stands from another perspective: for what they tell us about the universal problems he addresses in *Star Maker*.

Stapledon's battle with Ignotus came in 1935 and 1936, as Italy attacked and crushed Ethiopia, the League of Nations collapsed as a peacekeeping body, Germany occupied the Rhineland, and the Spanish Civil War broke out. In a letter of 3 November 1934 to the *Birkenhead News*, Stapledon called for international agreements to reduce armaments. He also took a position for collective security, saying that the League of Nations, although weak at present, is the only tool we have for containing aggressive nations. Thus, Stapledon called for the League to use economic and nonmilitary means to stop Italy and Germany, but to avoid military ones. He acknowledged that individual people *would* be justified in using force to stop a hooligan's attack, but he said that this individual aggression is not parallel to international aggression, for there is no international police force which can step in to control the violence. Moreover, using force against a hooligan affects only a few people, whereas using force against an aggressive nation may affect the whole world. Thus, Stapledon took a pacifist position but a flexible one that stressed relying on the League.

In letters of 4 August 1935 (*Sunday Mercury*, Birmingham) and 29 October 1935 (LDP), Stapledon made his stance gloomier and also cosmic. The West, he asserted, is in decline; air warfare would mean the end of civilization. The hope is that Britain can play a special role, a leading role in mediation. Stapledon again called on the League to apply economic sanctions to Italy, hoping that this action would bolster the League's admittedly low prestige. As for Britain, Stapledon called for unilateral disarmament, although he added that "I must recognize that such a course has no chance of being accepted at present." Stapledon then added a striking, perhaps startling point:

> Tentatively I favour, along with progressive disarmament and the development of the League, the creation of a small but well-equipped world air police, which, stationed at all danger-points, would *automatically* operate whenever international law was infringed, or threatened. (LDP, 29 October 1935)

Even though Stapledon then went on to acknowledge the dangers inherent in this proposal, his is a remarkable position for a pacifist. Before we look at Ignotus' response, let us pause to acknowledge the difficulties in what Stapledon was calling for. Granted, hindsight makes things clearer than they were in 1935, but even today World War II is more difficult for pacifists to take a position on than World War I, and Stapledon of course agonized over World War I, much less over the second war. One obvious problem with Stapledon's stance is to have advocated unilateral disarmament in the face of rising fascist armament, but Stapledon acknowledged that this position would not be accepted. A glaring contradiction exists, however, between opposing League military action and calling for a world air police to act "automatically." It is as though Stapledon were putting air warfare in a category different from other military action, much as we do today with nuclear weapons. The concept of automatic "world air police" makes one think of the film *Things to Come*, with Raymond Massey, representing the supranational "wings over the world," dressed in a black suit and flying in a futuristic airplane or, later, *The Day the Earth Stood Still*, in which Klatu, representing a race of seemingly pacifist aliens, warns Earth that in the event of aggression a race of Gort-like robots will automatically destroy the planet. Stapledon seems to be struggling to find military action which will transcend the moral difficulties of such action. Unfortunately, his call for "automatic," supranational response to aggression could work only if such aggression were discernable and unambiguous. But modern war often blurs this distinction, so that attack and defense look the same. One interpretation of the reason for the outbreak of World War I is that the allegedly "defensive" mobilizations could in fact be seen as offensive.

In his response to this letter (LDP, 31 October 1935), Ignotus surprisingly did not seize directly on Stapledon's calls for a world air police, other than to suggest that Stapledon's "solutions" were unlikely to come about for generations. Instead, Ignotus concentrated on Stapledon's view of the League as morally unfit for military action. Ignotus says:

> Yet this self-same League, without moral authority, and gravely suspect of self-interested motives, is to be allowed or even encouraged to "act vigorously" and apply "economic sanctions" which will leave a far deeper and more dangerous legacy of hatred than any armed attack. In short, the League can act without proper moral authority while it carries out Dr. Stapledon's particular wishes, but must wait for further backing before it ventures to carry out the wishes of those who differ from him....
>
> With the rest of Dr. Stapledon's letter, rather pathetic in its ineffectualness, there is no need to deal. (LDP, 31 October 1935)

I have quoted at length to convey something of the tone of Ignotus' letters—perhaps closer to sneer than to simple sarcasm. Rarely if ever does Ignotus divulge positions of his own; he concentrates, rather, on the logic of what Stapledon says. Accustomed as we perhaps are to thinking of Stapledon's positions as just and highminded, we may be surprised at Ignotus' vehement responses to them. In fairness, though, Ignotus often has the logical upper hand. If the League is gravely suspect, can it apply economic sanctions though not military ones? In general, a reasonable test of any proposition is whether there is a possibility of carrying it out, and for Stapledon's propositions, especially for a world air police, that possibility was often near zero.

As far as I can tell, Stapledon did not reply to Ignotus' first letter and for some time seemed reluctant to dignify Ignotus with any reply. But in March 1936 (LDP, 13 and 18 March), when Germany occupied the Rhineland, Stapledon stepped into a dispute between Captain Graham, M.P. for the Wirral, and Jean Absalom, who had pressed him for League sanctions. Graham objected to communists in the organization to which Absalom belonged, but Stapledon said he would work for just causes regardless of who was in the organizations fighting for them. In his stance toward German aggression,

Stapledon again walked a tightrope. He favored oil sanctions, but not military action. Critical of German fascism, he criticized Britain equally, objecting to the British government's rearmament policy. Indeed, Stapledon addressed himself as much to Britain as to Germany, stressing past British sins and claiming that envy of the British Empire is one cause of German aggression, so that all non-self-governing colonies should be brought under League control. Deeply critical of the German cult of state and race and German denial of civil liberties, Stapledon also feared that many in Britain would condone German behavior. Stapledon called for unconditional negotiations with Germany, adding that British rearmament shows Britain is not serious about international cooperation. And he added that Britain should "insist on a non-aggression pact between Germany and Russia" (LDP, 18 March 1936). This was one of Stapledon's proposals that *did* come about within a few years, arguably having the opposite effect that Stapledon intended, since the pact secured Hitler's eastern border and allowed him to attack westward in 1940.

When Professor Alan Dorward attacked the vagueness of Stapledon's proposals, Stapledon in a letter of 23 March 1936 (LDP) added a more specific point, calling for League occupation of the Maginot line and a strip of Germany, "*if only* France and Germany could be persuaded to accept." Thus, "if Germany, breaking pledges, attacks Eastern or the Central European states, the League (with France) can take action across the Rhine." History was not to unfold quite in this way, however. Perhaps Stapledon sensed the limitations of his own scheme when he added the following curious paragraph:

> If Professor Dorward exposes the weakness of this scheme, it will not be the first time that his diabolical intelligence has triumphed over my (approximately) divine innocence. (LDP, 23 March 1936)

Indeed, Stapledon described accurately the tone not only of his dispute with Dorward but with Ignotus.

And Dorward's sarcastic response was worthy of Ignotus. Stapledon's scheme, Dorward says, is "impossible to carry out," because the League is not a supranational body. Stapledon's letter, Dorward says, is "a brilliant work of the creative imagination; we expect this quality from the author of *Last and First Men*" (LDP, 27 March 1936).

On 5 May 1936, Italian forces occupied Addis Ababa, and Ethiopian resistance collapsed. Almost simultaneously, the main battle between Stapledon and Ignotus broke out. The dispute was touched off by Stapledon's remarks to the Hoylake League of Nations Union (reported in the LDP and *Birkenhead News* of 9 May) that, although a pacifist, he was willing to gamble that Italian sanctions would not mean war. Stapledon added that we must take the gamble, for Mussolini is "drunk with success."

In a 13 May letter to the LDP, Ignotus seized on Stapledon's statement about gambling, saying that Stapledon (as a typical pacifist) is prepared to risk war to establish pacifism; that those who have advocated peace now want to involve us in a war; and, worse, that these same people are unwilling to advocate steps that would make this war successful: military preparations and conscription. Stapledon's position, Ignotus concluded, is a "humiliating evasion."

On 18 May (LDP) Stapledon wrote his first response to Ignotus, taking up the challenge to state his position without "humiliating evasion," while nonetheless saying that "I refrain from textual criticism of his [Ignotus'] curious dissertation." That is, Ignotus attacked the logic of Stapledon's position with diabolical intelligence, but Stapledon in divine innocence refrained from a close look at Ignotus' logic, instead further explaining his own position, and in his honesty sometimes making it more rather than less vulnerable. First, Stapledon admitted there may be no solution to international aggression—at least not now, since the "heroic friendliness" of complete pacifism will not now be accepted. If his call for world air police had not made it clear, Stapledon's 18 May letter established that his earlier opposition to League military action had changed—though Stapledon does not directly acknowledge or explain the change. Thus Stapledon asks each state to put its forces at the League's disposal for action in the event of aggression:

> If the minimum League force was secured, Mussolini would not attack, or if, in crazy desperation, he did, the resulting hostilities would be decisive, brief, and relatively uncostly in terms of human life. Subsequently brigandage would seem unattractive. (LDP, 18 May 1936)

Such comments as these led Ignotus to redouble his attack in the LDP of 21 May. As well he might, Ignotus found Stapledon's statement amazing that war against Italy by a combination of powers could be brief and relatively uncostly (LDP, 21 May). Again Ignotus called on Stapledon to back up such a war with calls for military preparedness and conscription. Slyly, Ignotus adds a new dimension to the discussion by asking Stapledon what would be achieved by a League war against Italy, inasmuch as pacifists maintain that war settles nothing. Ignotus concluded that:

> Dr. Stapledon reminds one of a ship's officer who, in the midst of a disaster at sea, declines to say whether the boats are to be lowered, but invites us all to the saloon to hear a lecture by him on "The Problem of Safety at Sea, with Special Reference to Ships of the Future." (LDP, 21 May 1936)

Stapledon readers may well find this portion of the exchange with Ignotus painful to read, for Stapledon's efforts to escape Ignotus' spider webs of logic and sarcasm merely trap him further. Answering on 25 May (LDP), Stapledon took the dubious position that England is already spending enough on military preparedness (and likewise does not need conscription), repeated that war settles nothing "in the long run," and develops a dubious distinction between 1936 and 1914, for "in those days there was no real system of international order to defend." This seems to mean that today the rules of international order are so clear that the League can easily determine when they have been violated. Stapledon still wants unilateral disarmament, but is impressed with doing something with the forces we have.

Reacting to this last statement, Ignotus on 27 May (LDP) professed himself glad that Stapledon at last admits Britain can use its existing military strength, which need not be reduced. But Ignotus also hammered again at the point that if Stapledon is for collective security he must also be for conscription, as Britain's allies will not let our young men off. Ignotus added, with some reason, that sanctions against Italy were now a dead issue, Italy's conquest of Ethiopia being a *fait accompli*.

At the end of Ignotus' 27 May letter, the editor of the LDP announced that "this correspondence is now closed." Momentarily, Ignotus had had the last word, but the truce was to be a short one, for within a month Stapledon and Ignotus were at it again. In the interim, Stapledon defended himself from attack by another party, Eric Jones, and again attacked Captain Graham, M.P.; one wonders at times how Stapledon got any other work done. To explain the crisis facing democracy, Stapledon frequently discussed "gregism," the culture of the herd, as an important cause. Eric Jones assailed this concept, saying that Stapledon's "herd" is simply the unprivileged majority being driven by the privileged minority (LDP, 23 May 1936). While agreeing with Jones about privilege, Stapledon insisted that "gregism" may affect both the privileged and the unprivileged (LDP, 30 May 1936).

Attacking Captain Graham, Stapledon asserted anew that while the statement "war settles nothing" is not true in a literal sense (thus war does settle the lives of those killed), it is true in "essence." Stapledon made a surprisingly personal assessment of Captain Graham as being caught up in militarism psychologically, while underneath being a "wee cowering timorous beastie." Graham talks of defending London, said Stapledon, but there is no real defense. In any case, Germany's envy of the British Empire is the most important cause of war. Stapledon added, in a statement that seems as silly as it is close to what we now call appeasement, that "the one way to ensure that London shall not be bombed is to prove that we are not dangerous neighbours" (LDP, 12 June 1936). We must have the "courage to disarm."

This letter prompted Ignotus' response and a whole new round of exchanges that may be the most interesting part of the correspondence for those interested in theories of war and peace, for this round concerned the general question of whether war settles anything. Ignotus came up with wars that allegedly settled something: the American Revolution, the American Civil War, the Norman Conquest, and the conquest of Ethiopia—and he and Stapledon debated these wars one by one, in letter after letter. If Stapledon can reasonably be said to have lost the debate on League sanctions, he held his own here—though just barely—by replying specifically to Ignotus' arguments and by using sarcasm, two tactics he had previously avoided. Ignotus claimed that both the American Revolution and Civil War were triumphs of principle and that the Norman Conquest had enduring effects; Stapledon replied that the American Revolution and Civil War merely confirmed the inevitable trend of economic and historical forces, and that *effects* are not the same as *settlements*. Ignotus in turn replied that "Abraham Lincoln would have wilted under the implications of this professorial rebuke," meaning that those who take part in history feel themselves to be free and would read Stapledon's position as contrary to common sense (LDP, 29 June 1936). Hindsight certainly proclaims Stapledon the winner on Italy's conquest of Ethiopia, which Ignotus claimed to be as permanent as the Norman Conquest; but surely Ignotus makes an important point when he says that to say "war settles nothing" is meaningless, as no human problem is capable of final settlement.

The Stapledon-Ignotus debate switched to other matters and dragged on into the autumn of 1936, but generally with increasing diffidence and sarcasm. Here are some samples of Ignotus' letters:

> We do all so wish that Dr. Stapledon would cheer up. (LDP, 18 June 1936)

> Even Dr. Stapledon's friends must feel rather puzzled as to where he now stands. (LDP, 8 October 1937)

> He [Stapledon] says that he has not ceased to advocate disarmament. I *know* he has ceased to advocate it (or even to believe in it) as a practical policy for today. (LDP, 14 October 1936)

And here is a sample from Stapledon:

> "Ignotus," a heavy Puck, continues to disport himself by impishly misrepresenting honest mortals.... The pacific spirit is evidently beyond the range of the "Ignotian" mind. When argument sinks to vituperation, the best reply is merriment. (LDP, 12 October 1936)

In a more serious vein, on 3 November 1936 (LDP) Stapledon made both his final response to Ignotus and his best effort to show the consistency of his position. Rising to Ignotus' challenge that he had given up disarmament, Stapledon urged Britain to disarm, for "the British government is not fit to be trusted with an air gun, let alone an air force." Britain doesn't want collective security; "arms in their hands are likely to be a strength of reaction throughout the world."

Moveover, to arm against fascism would be to give fascism an excuse to arm against us; whereas, if Britain did disarm "with sincerity and resolution, Fascism would crumble and vanish, and the new age that we all desire would at last begin." But if Britain will not disarm, "we must make the best of a very bad job and at least work for international control of armaments." In sum, Stapledon had "no use for a pacifism that is too pure, too self-righteous, to compromise."

But by this point, unfortunately, Stapledon had compromised about all of his pacifism away. For example, on 23 October 1936 he was—by his own admission—making a common front with Winston Churchill in calling for an International Police Force. In a rare concession, Ignotus admitted on 8 October that Stapledon was trying to establish "some sort of common front between the whole-hog pacifists and the supporters of armaments" (LDP). Ignotus concluded that "this scheme, excellent in theory, is quite unrealisable in practice." With all hope of international control of armaments gone, Stapledon may have concluded the same, for his newspaper correspondence of the next three years makes hardly any reference to tactics for coping with the gathering storm. With the League discredited, Stapledon turned to a movement, in hindsight seemingly irrelevant, for federal union of the democratic countries. Only very abstractly did Stapledon construe federal union as relating to the immediate crisis, saying only that federal union would help destroy capitalism and that capitalism is the cause of war.

When Stapledon returned to the LDP with comments on current events, not until 7 July 1939, he made no reference to pacifism, disarmament, or federal union. Instead he attacked Chamberlain's discredited appeasement policy, fearing that Chamberlain might still be trying to deal secretly with Hitler. The only way to give credibility to the British government, he stressed, was to add Churchill to the cabinet. And when war did break out, Stapledon wrote (*South Wales Argus*, 5 September 1940) that this is a "war to settle what sort of society and what sort of morality shall be established in Europe, and ultimately in the world." What had happened to "war settles nothing"?

How far Stapledon had been forced to compromise his principles may be seen in a private letter he wrote to Naomi Mitchison on 10 July 1940. He spoke of hating all political work and added that:

> My (qualified) pacifism has been put in cold storage. But how loathsome it all is! And of course I remain fundamentally just as much pacifist as before. But at present pacifism simply won't work. I note in Gandhi's autobiography that his non-violence movement's success depended on the fact that some officials were decent folk. It would not have worked against a Nazi regime. (National Library of Scotland)

Stapledon's dreary tone confirms that, seen from one perspective, his public stance on the events of 1935–1940 was a failure. To repeat, the times were impossibly difficult and hindsight makes us wise. But Ignotus saw Stapledon's inadequate stance as symptomatic of the failure of a generation of intellectuals who, though "trained to strictly logical thought," are "as much at the mercy of their prejudices" as the average person when they enter a practical field (LDP, 31 October 1935). The pacifists, Ignotus said elsewhere, "are in a position to view the dismal failure of their excellently meant schemes" (LDP, 13 May 1936).

But seen from other perspectives, Stapledon's public stance in the late 1930s was successful. First and least important, Stapledon's letters look better when we remember that Ignotus hid behind a pseudonym and propounded few if any ideas. If nonviolence will not work now, said Stapledon, the reason is "too many 'Ignoti' who mistake lack of vision for common sense" (LDP, 18 May 1936). Perhaps, after all, there may be another side to Ignotus' lack of vision; while sarcastic about Stapledon, he seems at times to be implying that with Stapledon's training and ability he ought to be doing better. If this is an accurate reading, Stapledon would surely agree.

Stapledon's stand *was* inadequate; his ideas could not work in the 1930s; but he *did* proclaim a vision that may yet work—aspects of which *must* work if we are to save the world. Collective security, heroic friendliness—these are Stapledon's legacy. And without those who espouse causes that are at first impossible, the causes can never become possible. Stapledon was on the left; and as Leszek Kolakowski says of the "Concept of the Left,"

> [It] is the fermenting factor in even the most hardened mass of the historical present. Even though it is at times weak and invisible, it is nonetheless the dynamite of hope that blasts the dead load of ossified systems, institutions, customs, intellectual habits, and closed doctrines. The Left unites those dispersed and often hidden atoms whose movement is, in the last analysis, what we call progress. (83)

Finally, the stance of Stapledon the public man—the third Stapledon—becomes mediated into the work of the more familiar first Stapledon, the writer of *Star Maker*, on which he was struggling at the same time that he was struggling with Ignotus. In the last paragraph of *Star Maker*, Stapledon speaks of *two* lights for guidance, one of them "our little glowing atom of community," with all of its 1930s sense of world crisis. Stapledon needed the concrete struggle with Ignotus to express the wider struggle taking place among "the cold light of the stars." Stapledon only lived to be sixty-four, and he spent an enormous amount of time dealing with issues which may now seem to us dated and futile. Had he spent all of his time on artistic creation, how much more might he have done? As in other respects, there may be a parallel with Milton here, "wasting" his creative energy on lost political causes. Stapledon's avowed socialism may even be a reason, particularly in the United States, for the rapid decline of his reputation in the 1950s. Yet Milton's politics found their way into his creative works, and so did Stapledon's. Although *Star Maker* is no allegory of the 1930s, Stapledon deconstructs these affairs as he knew and participated in them, transforming them in a number of ways. Sometimes he universalizes the particular things he saw; sometimes he says the opposite of what he was saying in his letters.

For example, in the "Other Earth," the first world to be visited by the pilgrims in *Star Maker*, Stapledon takes the effect of the mass media seriously by satirizing them, thus confirming that he believed that responding to Ignotus in the mass media was important. For the "Other Men" have developed "radio bliss" to the point that it can directly stimulate brain centers, so that eventually "a man could retire to bed for life and spend all his time receiving radio programmes" (*SM* 3:279–80). And in many ways *Star Maker* develops themes we have been examining in the LDP. For instance, we may remember the "mad worlds" of chapter 9, "The Community of Worlds." Even as it seems that the galaxy is about to become an awakened utopia, Stapledon presents the tragic case of those

> more awakened worlds whose obsession was seemingly for community itself and mental lucidity itself.... I have spoken as though I were confident that these formidable worlds were indeed mad, aberrant from the line of mental and spiritual growth. But their tragedy lay in the fact that, though to their opponents they seemed to be either mad or at heart wicked, to themselves they appeared superbly sane, practical, and virtuous. There were times when we ourselves, the bewildered explorers, were almost persuaded that this was the truth. (*SM* 9:356)

It is difficult to read this passage without imagining Stapledon's outlook on Ignotus. Stapledon speaks of the "fixation" of the waking worlds on their current planes of endeavour, "so that no further advance could occur" (*SM* 9:352), much as Ignotus was intelligent about the present but misguided about future developments. And was not Stapledon a "bewildered explorer" in the 1930s, at times almost persuaded by the diabolical intelligence of an Ignotus and bewildered too about how to respond to both Soviet Russia and fascism?

When the pilgrims of *Star Maker* note the spreading attacks of those worlds that are "mad" with their overzealousness for community, the narrator connects us with what the public Stapledon was fighting for in the 1930s, telling us that "I was forcibly reminded of the state of bewilderment and anxiety that I had left behind me on the Earth" (*SM* 9:359–60). To further connect his readers to the political world of the 1930s, Stapledon has his ordinary sane worlds organize "into a League to resist aggression" (*SM* 9:360), a league as futile as the League of Nations that Stapledon struggled to support at the same time that Italy's triumph liquidated it.

But as the "mad worlds"—read Mussolini and Hitler—are about to triumph, Stapledon develops the special role of the Symbiotics, "those brilliant Ichthyoid and Arachnoid Symbiotics who played a leading part in the history of our galaxy" (*SM* 9:352). Representing the union of opposites, the Symbiotics give us what did not happen but would have needed to happen to bring a happier outcome to 1930s events. For in the wars between the two species the superior power of the Arachnoids does not win; instead, fraternization between the two species leads to a symbiotic species that is higher than either, a species that, living in an "outlying 'island' off the galactic 'continent' " is able to defeat the mad worlds militarily but refuses to do so, even though the attacking mad worlds destroy three advanced worlds who meet their fate with "exaltation and inner peace" (*SM* 9:362–63). Finally the Symbiotics subvert the mad worlds telepathically, spreading the " 'disease' of sanity" to large populations on the mad worlds (*SM* 9:369). At last the mad worlds are brought to sanity, but not before extensive violence and civil war.

Again, Stapledon could not have written these passages without the political stands he was taking. He wanted a special role for Britain, another island off another continent, in combating madness, not by military means but by risking peace and disarmament. But Britain lacked the integration of the Symbiotics, who turned the differences between Arachnoids and Ichthyoids into strength; in Britain the splits between classes, between pacifists and militarists, made for weakness. The Symbiotics are largely a version of what Stapledon would have wanted for Britain. What the Symbiotics do, though, is in part also an inversion of what Stapledon said he wanted. True, they avoid a military response, and they bring peace—but at the cost of civil war. In the 1930s, Stapledon worked to stop conflict; but with the Symbiotics, as John Kinnaird points out, "world conflict is the necessary precondition for Utopian world-community" (70).

Other hostile situations in *Star Maker* receive a more pacific resolution. In wars between species of composite insects, swarms of tiny beings linked telepathically into intelligent creatures, key minds on each side preach peace and "the pacific races had the courage to disarm" (*SM* 7:333), daring to do what Stapledon hoped England would do. This passive resistance overcomes the aggressive species and produces a world federation. On Earth, Stapledon reminds us, "such a happy issue of strife is impossible, simply because the capacity for community in the individual mind is still too weak" (*SM* 7:334). Stapledon's gloom about Earth presumably has something to do with narrow and warlike Ignoti. And later in *Star Maker* the pilgrims become aware of a conflict between planets and their stars. The pilgrims discover that stars are living, intelligent organisms, who gradually become aware that their planets contain intelligent life. Two parties develop among the stars about the minded planets. The first party—and initially the largest—sees them as diabolical, much as the many Ignoti see England's enemies. But a minority party wants peace and symbiosis with the planets, and this party finally achieves a galactic symbiosis of stars and planetary systems. In all these situations—Symbiotics versus the mad worlds, wars between species of insects, and conflict between stars and worlds—Stapledon gives us variations on the same themes that preoccupied him in the struggle with Ignotus.

Any doubt that *Star Maker* is in one sense a commentary on the 1930s vanishes in the "Epilogue: Back to Earth," in which Stapledon describes his era as an "age of titanic conflict" (*SM* Epilogue: 431). Stapledon sees the Earth as an arena for "two cosmical antagonists, two spirits," one of them, surely the spirit of Ignotus, characterized by "the myopic fear of the unknown" (*SM* Epilogue: 433). Facing this narrow spirit of the past is the "will to dare for the sake of the new"—a spirit willing to try anything to avoid world catastrophe, as Stapledon was in his letters to the LDP, whether the desired experiment be, first, disarmament, and later—when disarmament was no longer a possibility—international control of armaments, Italian sanctions, or even a world air force.

Thus the correspondence with Ignotus, seemingly remote from the frosty ecstasy of *Star Maker*, is really the flip side of the same coin. Stapledon's political work provided part of the outlook and subject matter for his creative work. Finally, Stapledon's political work is important to us as an example. At times, at least, Stapledon hated political work, but he knew he had to do it—and he was correct. I've shown the contradictory and inadequate nature of much of what he did, but to engage in political struggle is to be contradictory and inadequate. Kolakowski has a chapter entitled "In Praise of Inconsistency." Even the compromises Stapledon tried to make, while at the same time holding as fast as he could to principle, should set us to thinking. Faced with nuclear winter and imperialism, faced with the West's complicity in South African racism, faced with the poverty and decay of U.S. cities and the political struggles in modern Liverpool, academics and others would do well to remember that Stapledon found the time to fight the day's battles.

WORKS CITED

Kinnaird, John. *Olaf Stapledon*. [Starmont Reader's Guide, 21] Mercer Island, Wash.: Starmont House, 1986.

Kolakowski, Leszek. *Toward a Marxist Humanism*. Trans. Jane Zielonko Peel. New York: Grove, 1968.

7

Olaf Stapledon's "Letters to the Future"

Robert Crossley, editor

(To Robert, Christopher, Emma, Adam, and Matthew Stapledon, Great-grandchildren of Olaf Stapledon)

Because Olaf Stapledon's fame rests chiefly on scientific and philosophical romances of stunningly impersonal scope, bizarre invention, and densely clinical language, it may seem perverse to claim that the literary form most essential to him was the familiar letter. Stapledon, after all, wrote just one epistolary novel, *The Flames*, which is short enough to be called a novella and consists mostly of a single long letter. By the standards of the eighteenth-century epistolary novelists he hardly qualifies as a contender. But he was himself a prodigious letter-writer from the age of six, when he was separated from his father who continued working at the Suez Canal after young Olaf and his mother left Egypt for Liverpool. For ten years he wrote weekly to his father, and soon added other correspondents to his list.[1] Barely a year after his father rejoined the family in Liverpool in 1901, Olaf departed for boarding school and again he had to depend on letters to and from his family.

By the time he reached his early twenties Stapledon's correspondence had grown hugely, and his most remarkable early writings are the million and a half words of courtship letters he dispatched between 1910 and 1919 to his Australian cousin Agnes Miller, a fraction of which have been printed. Often in that correspondence he talked explicitly about the epistolary genre. Some letters are "slapdash and like a single coat of paint on a subject";[2] but "the ideal letter," he once wrote, "is the clear record of a particular thought-train."[3] One striking definition will delight readers who recall both the presence of Agnes Stapledon and the image of the pulsating lighthouse in the first and last chapters of *Star Maker*: in 1911 he told Agnes how letters "are like the dim point of light in a distant lighthouse between the bright flashes of the revolving light."[4] Among his lost manuscripts from the World War I years were an intended work of philosophical fiction based on his own correspondence with Agnes and an epistolary novel for workingmen organized as letters to and from the front.[5] During World War II he started an imaginary civilian-soldier correspondence, *Letters to a Militiaman*, the manuscript of which resides in the Stapledon Archive at the University of Liverpool. Even after his literary career was well-established, he remained an indefatigable author of letters to newspaper editors on a variety of subjects—mostly political and ethical—as Curtis Smith has shown in his contribution to the present volume.

In the summer of 1917, while at home on brief leave from the Friends' Ambulance Unit, Stapledon enclosed in a long letter to his fiancée a charming set of notes dated at various points in time. The last of the four enclosures, written in his tiny and precise script, is addressed "TO AGNES IN THE YEAR 1999" and is one of the earliest surviving examples of his lifelong and frequently whimsical preoccupation with time and posterity:

> Dearest,
>
> It will be all over when you get this. This war will be over, & you and I will be over. What we two shall be then, I don't know. But if we do live in some way or other, and can remember and feel, then we will be lovers still. Perhaps you smile at this letter, & perhaps I also must smile at it in 1999. But I in 1917, in the middle of all these wars and wonders, set down as a certain thing that for you & for me both then & now the main thing in all the world is that we love one another.
>
> For ever
> Your Olaf[6]

This was Stapledon's first letter to the future, his first effort to speak from beyond the grave, speculating how the world might look from that vantage, wondering what would persist and what would fail in the final winnowing of a life.

The literary conceit of a disembodied voice, speaking across gulfs of time and defying both physics and mortality, figures most extravagantly in *Last and First Men*, but it animates others of Stapledon's works, including the radio script "Far Future Calling," the science-fictional Bildungsroman *Last Men in London*, the cosmological quest *Star Maker*, and the World War II fantasy *Death into Life*. The telepaths in *Odd John* represent a special case of disembodied communication, and Stapledon himself from his youth to his last years took an interest—both theoretical and practical—in experiments with telepathy. Everywhere in his fiction there appear hopeful adventurers launching messages in bottles that may wash up someday and find a fit reader who will grasp the urgency of the communication; thus the freakish *enfant terrible* Odd John, anticipating an early death, urges his biographer to tell his story to posterity, and the inmate of the asylum in *The Flames* calls on an old university friend to publish to the world his lengthy prophetic letter about "a kind of future which we do not at all desire" (*Flames* 61). The concern to affect posterity by leaving a lasting testament can be found not only in Stapledon's longer fictions but in his pastiche of autobiography and sociology called *Youth and Tomorrow*, in the chapter on the future he wrote for Naomi Mitchison's children's encyclopedia,[7] and in his utopian pamphlet *Old Man in New World*.

Throughout Stapledon's work there runs a grand paradox: an imaginative attraction to large, inhuman vistas of time and space is recurrently set against private anxieties about human brevity. Friends used to observe his strikingly youthful appearance, even in his forties and fifties, by calling him a "Peter Pan," and the Divine Boy in *Last and First Men* is surely an ironic self-study. But Stapledon had no illusions that he could cheat time. "Old age is upon the young man's heels," he wrote in an early poem,[8] and indeed his literary celebrity, achieved at the ripe age of forty-four, was cruelly brief. Shortly before his death he wrote of himself as "the aging man, who with new eyes sees his small triumphs as failures" (*OE* 3:4). Sometime in the late 1940s—perhaps just after his first grandson was born in 1948—he explored the notion of leaving behind some letters addressed specifically to his own great-grandchild. The manuscript was never completed, but it gives abundant, often eloquent, testimony of Stapledon's desire to peer into the near future just beyond his own mortal boundary and to transmit the central tenets of his vision to his descendants. As the tentative dedication on the earliest surviving page of draft suggests, his ultimate aim was to speak not only to a member of his own family but to an entire future generation: "to those who will be young when we are dead."

Much of Stapledon's imagined communication with his great-grandson echoes the central issues of his fiction and his social criticism. When, for instance, near the opening of the first letter he justifies his exercise in speaking to a different era on the grounds that "it is salutary to judge ourselves through the eyes of the future," he offers essentially the very rationale that underpins the fictional premise of *Last and First Men*. Similarly, the discussion in Letter II of the difficulty of reconciling self-consciousness with "other-regarding impulses" recalls his persistent concern in other writings with the psychological and the social imperatives in human development—what he called "personality-in-community." The image of human history as a fugue, evocations of stars and electrons and birds and butterflies, rhetorical strategies of opposition and apparent contradiction: all these stylistic features of the letters come from the common store out of which Stapledon always furnished his prose. And there are allusions to some of his familiar touchstones: in Letter I, to J. D. Bernal, author of *The World, the Flesh, and the Devil*, and William Blake, the "prophet" in revolt against the Ancient of Days; to the legacies of Socrates and Jesus in Letters II and III; and to Whitehead ("one of our philosophers") in Letters III and IV.

But if *Letters to the Future* offers a gloss on some old Stapledonian themes of the 1930s, it also provides revealing glimpses into his final years, when disillusionment with his own faltering career lent a sweetly melancholic autobiographical flavor to his writings, and when the state of world politics drove him to increasingly hortatory rhetoric about the future. *Letters to the Future* belongs to the same creative stage as Stapledon's articles and addresses on nuclear power and world peace and his most transparently self-referential works since *Last Men in London*: *A Man Divided* and the posthumous *Opening of the Eyes* and *Four Encounters*.[9] His claim in Letter I that his "very obscurity" might qualify him better than more famous writers to speak for the mid-twentieth century reflects his loss of publicity after 1943, when all his old books went out of print and he began having trouble securing publishers for his new works. In the final letter, as he muses on "the fate of all mediocre minds when they over-reach their stature," the self-assessment is excruciating. Many of Stapledon's last works are elegiac in mood, almost as if he had a premonition of early death; in the interludes of *Death into Life* and the luminous, recently discovered allegory "The Peak and the Town," as in *Letters to the Future*, there is a mournful nostalgia for his youth, his creative achievements, and his brief public renown.[10] The Stapledon of *Letters to the Future* is warier than the author of *Last and First Men*. He is, in the aftermath of a second world war quite different from the one he imagined in 1930, reluctant to predict very much about the coming age: the future recipient of the four letters might read them amid the comforts of a civilization poised to embark on a sane new twenty-first century, or he might puzzle out Stapledon's words while sitting in the rubble of a demolished world. The author who bravely espied humanity two billion years hence in *Last and First Men* now cannot see clearly half a century ahead.

Nevertheless, though modest in tone, *Letters to the Future* is a forthright confession of faith from a secular evangelist earnestly sending epistles to fin de siècle civilization—if any such thing remains. In counseling his great-grandson to a "radical Worldliness" rather than soul-saving, Stapledon stresses his commitments as a social reformer, commitments sometimes blurred by the emphasis on spiritual vision in his early fiction. Without abandoning his consistently held view that self-cultivation and social conscience are inseparable in the fully mature and awakened person, Stapledon makes clearer than ever before the "religion of worldliness" to which he called his initial readers and which still has power to move and to persuade new readers forty years after the author's death, even as his oldest great-grandchildren enter early adulthood. The existence of the manuscript of *Letters to the Future* dramatically illustrates Stapledon's literary ambition to speak to, for, and about future humanity and things to come, but it also testifies to the special vitality of all texts that find an audience beyond their authors' lifetimes. That vitality is identified by Stapledon's great forebear in epic, polemic, and visionary modes, Milton, who insisted that "a good book is the precious lifeblood of a master spirit, embalmed and treasured up on purpose to a life beyond life."[11] Unsealed after forty years, these letters retain the freshness of the master spirit that composed them.

The printed text of *Letters to the Future* derives from the best available holograph version of each letter. The earliest draft, titled *A Letter to the Future*, contemplates a single long letter, but that plan quickly yielded to a multiple-letter structure. Stapledon appears to have composed the first three letters in order, but then to have grown dissatisfied with the second and third, intending to drop them. What is published here as Letter IV Stapledon at one point designed to replace Letter II. He then, however, started rewriting the earlier version of Letter II and restored its original number, suggesting a probable return to his scheme of four letters. Letter II exists in two forms, one of which is complete; the printed text relies on the second, incomplete revision but reverts to the earlier manuscript for the missing final portion. The fourth letter was never finished. It exists in a brief, patchy version, and a longer, more detailed one which stops abruptly; the latter has been adopted as copy-text. Beyond that it is impossible to guess Stapledon's intentions or his reasons for giving up the letters. He did annotate all four letters in his habitual method for revising manuscripts, indicating passages to be cut, interpolations, and stylistic alterations. I have adopted all such manuscript changes on the assumption that they represent Stapledon's final thoughts before he abandoned the project.[12]

LETTERS TO THE FUTURE

From an Age of Perplexity

LETTER I

A letter of introduction.
To my Great Grandson in early manhood.

Sir,

If ever you come upon this letter, forgive its preglacial dialect, and have patience to spell out its meaning. How gladly would I address you in whatever speech lives in your ears! The thoughts which follow must, I know, reach you only as dead and fragile specimens; but today they live. They flit among us dazzlingly and elusively, and we fight about them; for some of us fear them as the plague and would exterminate them, while others prize them as the light of our world.

I will not forget that I can give you only a few dead butterflies of thought, and that perhaps you will be interested in them only because they will have become extinct. Nor will I forget that I have no personal claim on your respect. Far from it; I fear you will have to suffer for my follies, even as your world must suffer for the immense follies of mine. Our misconduct must remain inexcusable in your eyes, for it has been disreputable; and you are young. But I must also bear in mind the possibility that you may censure not only our admitted errors but even the most admired achievements of our time, and that you may dismiss as worthless our most cherished dogmas. I will try not to forget this possibility even on the wave-crest of confidence.

But in the trough I must be allowed to remind myself that we stand to be judged finally not by your age but by that fully informed mind (if ever there be such) which alone can have reason to claim certainty for its verdicts. Even you have authority only in so far as you approximate to that ideal.

If I do not propose to apologize for my own errors or the barbarism of an era, what purpose, you wonder, have I in burrowing up from oblivion into your day. It is inconceivable that a voice out of this grave of lost causes should offer you advice.

I might of course plead that I am writing not strictly for you but for myself; for it is salutary to judge ourselves through the eyes of the future. Or again, I might, and indeed I must, plead an innocuous kind of family affection which prompts me to interest myself in your affairs. But I have already learnt enough from one of your grandparents to know that this sentiment must be firmly controlled, lest it should develop into a passion for meddling in matters which a parent necessarily cannot understand. I promise you, then, I will be on my guard in this respect. I will frequently remind myself that a parent, and still more a great grandparent, is, in the nature of the case, out of date and naively ignorant; and that your wisdom loses mine in its pocket like a threepenny bit. Alas! You have doubtless long ago abolished that exasperating coin, and our petty wisdom also. Well, threepence has a certain potency whatever its form; and so I insist on slipping this right into your pocket.

I have more serious reasons for seeking contact with you. How should I *know* that your world will be more enlightened than mine? Today we find little reason to prophesy a millennium for you. Our own blunders seem to forbid it. Moreover even if, as we cannot but hope, you have somehow won through in spite of us, and can afford to smile at our little wisdom, it is well that I should speak to you. For this age, in spite of its bewilderment and disillusionment and obvious failure, has not been wholly without vision. In our darkness we begin to glimpse something whose nature (if it is as we suppose) demands that we record our view of it even at the risk of earning ridicule from a shrewder generation. This dawning apprehension, I venture to think, is more characteristic of our age than the disillusionment which we consciously affect. True we are but rarely and vaguely aware of this thing. Many of us never glimpse it at all. Not one among us has a clear view of it. But more and more of us, I believe, begin to turn toward it; and already for many it is the undiscovered goal toward which their best thought leads.

Do not fear that I shall urge you to seek God and save your soul, or preach a crusade against contraception or false teeth. Probably in your enlightenment you are as happily ignorant of these two latter clumsy but merciful dodges as you are emancipated from soul-saving and from the obsession with God. If not, for God's sake, sir, damn your soul and have done with it,—if you suppose yourself to have one; and so see the world more clearly, and enjoy it more shrewdly, and be more inclined to save *it*. For it is the world, and not his soul, that claims a man's attention and his care. It is *this* world of lands and seas, cornfields and cities, of jelly-fish and flies and chickweed, of pigs in their sties and roving gulls, of miners and profiteers and thinkers and screaming babies, of armies, trade unions, colleges, prisons, and panic-stricken nations, of electrons and multitudinous streams of suns, of applied maths and aesthetic and moral experience. What need to seek heaven for the ghost that a man supposes himself to be, when all these vivid and needy realities clamour around him?

Did I so far lack humour as to preach to you, I think I should exhort you to a radical Worldliness. I should urge, not pietism, but a whole-hearted devotion to the world, yes and to the flesh and the devil; but especially to the flesh, which bears all our spiritual sky-scrapers on its back as a soldier bears lice, but also to the devil since he is in reality.

But (thus I would preach if I dared) you must more than dally with this great trinity. You must be intimate with flesh till you know its very essence. And its very essence is after all a spirit, an attitude, an adventurousness toward it knows not what, and a delighted discovery of the world, and a tireless creativeness. This (I would affirm) is its essence, and not that mechanical and tyrannous routine of pleasure and pain in which it has become entangled, that vast back-water in which so much of life's torrent is forever trapped. Your worldliness, too, must exclude nothing. It must be at home not only in the West End but the East End, not only there but behind the Pole Star. And the devil you must know intimately before you claim to understand him. Then (as one of the prophets has shown) you will find him to be that bold and insolent spirit who has crept into this clod, our Earth, to quicken it into intelligent revolt against the Ancient of Days and his trivial round.

Of course if you are thorough with this religion of worldliness you will find yourself worshipping at the very same shrine as all honest men have ever frequented. But you will have stripped it of all vulgar tinsel, revealing the grey stone. And therefore many will have a secret grudge against you. For many are comforted by a painted surface even while they know it covers carved granite.

If you should fail to be thorough in your Worldliness, damned you will certainly be; and the pure in face will hound you. What is worse you will leave a mess behind you. But those who are half-hearted even in a more respectable faith leave filthy traces, traces the more poisonous for being tolerated and never mopped up.

In some such vein as this might I preach you as good a half-truth as ever became a slogan. But it is only half the truth. And moreover preaching won't go down with one's relatives. So I will make a plain tale of my faith, and temper it with many queries. For obviously we who believe may be mistaken. You perhaps will have already exposed our error and set our altar in your museum. Indeed even today certain clever young persons are trying to budge it. They think, I suppose, that because so many goods have gone bad on our hands goodness itself must be illusory. Well, they may prove right in the end; but meanwhile we find some amusement in watching them apparently tugging in vain at the rock face. Whether they are right or wrong they have not yet convinced us. We still believe, and must act on our belief. Folly is less shameful than disloyalty.

But it may well seem inappropriate that I, whose career has been a texture of good luck and bad management, should undertake to be the spokesman of an age which, whatever its failings, has not been inarticulate. I speak, however, as kinsman to kinsman, hoping that something of the family mannerism may render me intelligible to you when our more public voices have already become archaic. Further it is just possible that my very obscurity may fit me to speak more faithfully for my period than any of its great unique personalities.

But how can I write cogently to one with whom I am not even acquainted? Are you rich with the culture of your age, or are you a boor or a philistine? Are you curious about the nature of things, or content to see no further than your own food and the curves of woman? I cannot know; but I shall presume that you have the broad interests that are not uncommon in our family, and (like the rest of us) a certain capacity of reasoning. If you have not, it is to be hoped that you will at least have the sense to hand this letter, and those which follow, to someone of intelligence,—if there be any such alive in your day.

For in ours it is impossible to be sure that the human mind is not destroying itself. We seem to ourselves to be in a unique crisis of this planet's history,—a crisis which may soon end, or may, we suspect, drag on even far beyond the lives of your remote descendants. We are accustomed to describe man's present plight thus. His knowledge and power have lately increased extravagantly. His mind is embracing regions hitherto unguessed; and he can give effect to his will as never before. But these wide and deep discoveries, which should enlighten him as to what is truly desirable, do not in general have any influence on his choice of ends. He is ruled almost entirely by his animal and ancestral nature. He behaves very seldom in the manner that is uniquely human. Quite rightly he seeks the fulfillment of bodily and personal needs; and he even knows how to subordinate these to ends deemed more important; but his remoter ends are not as a rule chosen rationally, and are seldom objectively valid. He can transcend his private needs only for outworn or mistaken ideals imposed by ancestral taboos. For these alone are backed up by the forces of habit and public opinion.

Few of us today have seen what man is and what he might become. And of these, fewer see the starry universe as anything more than the stage of man's drama. Even when we glimpse the things that are better than food and sex and applause, and better than all the virtues, we cannot long act in conformity with our vision. Very soon we succumb to the old cravings or the old sightless conscience. And so the great power that we are acquiring issues in disaster. And no one knows what will become of his own children in the stupid riot.

There seem to us three possibilities with regard to the world in your time. Either the interest of the mass of men and women will have definitely passed beyond the puerile ends which infect us, and a new epoch will be dawning in the life of this planet; or, like us, you will continue to be at heart no more than anthropoid. The latter is the more probable alternative. And if this is the case, either civilization will still be hanging by a thread, or it will be already shattered.

I may then be addressing one whose society will have crashed into a second barbarism before ever it has achieved true civilization, one who may perhaps regard us (if he knows of us at all) with the misunderstanding adulation so often lavished on a more intelligent past. Or I may be exposing myself to one who will really be of a finer mentality than has yet been achieved on this planet, and to an age that has at last won through to some agreed certainty of belief and some unquestionable judgment as to the good, and to full sanity of will. Or again you, like us, may be more than animal yet not fully human, seeing fitfully the good, but unable to serve it with any constancy. Such I expect will be your state; though if you have not actually crashed you must surely have outgrown some of our follies. Sanity of thought and sanity of will may not be quite so rare with you as with us. Persons of common intelligence will perhaps be less entangled in the maze of superstitions from which none of us today can entirely escape.

If you have outstripped us even thus far you will scarcely be able to conceive our mental confusion. For today every hoax finds some believer, and every truth is obscured by a fog of argument. While some pathetically dress up old idols in modern clothes, others are naively disillusioned because they have ransacked the universe in vain for a trace of God. Yet all the while (if I mistake not) in the streets and the farms, and indeed in every span of every man's experience, something cries out for our admiration and our help, something better than any idol, something lovelier than the God of our fathers.

It is about this something that I must speak to you, lest your apprehension of it should through some misfortune happen to be more uncertain even than my own. But if when you read these letters you find that you have already passed beyond their range of thought, perhaps they will at least interest you historically; and perhaps you will forgive my importunity. However remote we may be from each other in time and in mentality, we are kin, and our two worlds are one. We, and all men, however gravely we conflict, are engaged on the same enterprise. In my language the goal of that enterprise may be called the fulfillment of the world's capacity; but if this sounds barbarous to you, call it what you will, so long as you recognize in me a fellow-worker, though far-removed.

LETTER II

A historical letter

Great Grandson,

If ever you wade through my first letter, will you, I wonder, take the plunge into my second? One thing, I fancy, will have amused you and may entice you further. I claimed in effect that an ethical conflict was the peculiarity of this age. But after all it is characteristic of every age; and if in your time some of our discords are resolved, others inconceivable to us must surely have arisen. In every age man has been discovering new ends that were intrinsically better than his accustomed ends, and has always been failing to wean his heart from the familiar and lesser good for the sake of the newly discovered better. Never before today, perhaps, has the process been so dramatic; for the customary habit of man's will has never before been so completely stultified by his increasing knowledge yet so reluctant to be transformed.

And because of the complexity and harshness of our conflicts we, perhaps more clearly than other ages, see the full irony of man's fate. For he does in the end succeed in disciplining himself to the new-found value and reshaping his whole manner of life,—but only to find that the precious thing is itself eclipsed by some yet higher excellence. Or in other cases the world is so changed that the hard-won value is revealed as but a means to an end, and no longer serviceable. And so he must either wrench the whole current of his life into a new channel, or, accepting means for end, pursue a phantom. How often in the career of each one of us has enthusiasm been followed by cold enlightenment or by reluctant recognition of some higher and almost repellent goal! How often in man's history has a new habit of will or a new ideal been painfully acquired by one generation only to be reviled and combatted by the next!

At this point a mockingly unctuous voice within me, (perhaps it is the voice that will be yours) sings from a song that will never be heard in your day, "Excelsior!" But do not deride me! I am not lapsing into moralism. I am not preaching a moral duty of climbing for climbing's sake, or for the sake of a heaven at the top. Let us be clear on this point. I refer only to the dire fact that familiar goods ever tend to reveal, as implicated in their own goodness, unfamiliar and better goods. Climb we must; but not merely to exercise our moral limbs; rather, (to pursue the image) because our presence is imperiously demanded on the summit; or because on the cliff face there is no rest, and to descend were treason, not to ourselves but to the spirit of the crags, the spirit to whom we pledged ourselves in our earliest act of admiration. We all admire something or other, whether a punch from the shoulder or the precise dancing of electrons. And whatever our admiration begins upon, it is led on, or should be led on, willy nilly to other things; and perhaps (as many philosophers have declared) it should logically advance to admiration of the Whole.

Perhaps the supreme instance of this advance to new values is the revolution which must have occurred when the race first gained self-consciousness, and is repeated in each child. Today it is so easy for us to value the "self" that no one takes credit for it. On the contrary, selfishness is on all hands condemned. But care for an enduring individuality rather than for the fleeting pleasures that it tastes were not always familiar. In that forgotten era when our animal ancestors first glimpsed themselves as "selves" how stubbornly must the old automatic self-less behaviour have resisted control by self-consciousness! Yet now, though we all have lapses even from this lowly plane, only infants and idiots live constantly the life of uncontrolled impulse, and have no habit whatever of self-value.

If you should ask what I mean by "self" I should have to remain silent, or embark on a course of inconclusive lectures. Suffice it that I mean that which experiences, endures through its experiences, and is distinct from others of its kind. But what that *is*, God knows. Perhaps it is the body "in its psychological aspect." Or perhaps, on the contrary, the body is but the physical aspect of self. What matter,—so long as we realise that each is nothing without the other.

Let me return to my theme. Even in the very age when ego was first discovered and valued and painfully preserved, our ancestors must have been apprehending not only themselves but their fellows as good. Long before self-respect was established, selfishness must have become a reproach. Irony! Love was impossible till there was knowledge of personality; but this no man could know till he was aware on the one hand of the distinction between himself and others, and on the other of the enduring unity of all his experiences; and affection for his own individuality, through which alone he could know others as persons, has itself been the great cause of his failure to embrace his neighbours also within the bright circle of his interest. Yet long before the dawn of self-consciousness man's behavior was already crowded with other-regarding impulses which pointed the way to conscious love, but which the blinkered devotée of ego must reject as irrelevant to his abstract and impossible ideal.

Man's career has indeed been a fugue whose theme, (the birth, struggle, triumph and eclipse of successive ideals), has been repeated in endless variety. While our ancestors were discovering themselves and their neighbours they began to notice also the unity of the social group, and to take society itself as an end. And in addition, even in that early time, they began to have glimpses, (many would say illusions), of value altogether extrahuman, superhuman, cosmical. And from the conflict of these diverse kinds of excellence sprang many ideals, all justified as instrumental to one or other of the prime goods, but each apt to be mistaken as an end and pursued to the exclusion of all else.

Forgive me if I weary you with matter already familiar. I must review my foundations before declaring my faith. Besides,—how can I know that you have ever thought at all about this progressive discovery of values, or that you see its tragic but glorious significance? (For it suggests, does it not?, that all that we deem most precious may, in the universal view, be utterly negligible.)

Consider the fate of the moralistic ideals. From the clash of the social and the private values, and not wholly from egoistic fear of governors, arose the concept of a law which *must* be obeyed. For when the group came to be regarded as itself a good thing it was obvious that, for the cohesion of the group, individuals must conform to certain principles of conduct whatever the consequences to themselves. This in fact is clearly the rational basis and the actual strength of law, whether it is recognized or not. And because of its social utility law became an established institution. But no sooner was law-abidingness recognized as a "virtue" than it began to be actually a vice. For law was mistaken as an end in itself. Outworn commandments, once perhaps of use, crystallized into a rigid and irrational taboo; and men imposed on themselves and on each other a thousand ludicrous disabilities, such as sabbatarianism and the ritual of prudery.

Thus arose the notion of the "virtues," the depressing view that the greatest good in the universe is willing conduct in accordance with certain rules. I shall not forget the joy with which my slow mind first discovered that the human race and the stars are not a poultry farm for the production of moral foie gras for a gluttonous God. Truthfulness and chastity and the like were revealed as only more sacred than a good style in tennis because they served a greater end. So it seemed at least to my youthful confidence. But what is the end? Is it perhaps, as in tennis, an action, but an act of the whole real?

We of today, even we, have outgrown the "virtues"; but there is a kindred illusion which has some power over us. All external rules stand to be criticized and often condemned by the private conscience, which claims to be superior to foreign authority. And obviously it is so; each man must judge right and wrong for himself and *choose* his own moral authorities. But conscience itself is but a blind groping after the desirable end; and the dictates of conscience, when they are but vague feelings of right and wrong, must be criticized. Conscientiousness, the following of our established conscience, cannot itself be the end, for conscience presupposes an objective distinction between good and bad. A man may conscientiously do great hurt to that which alone is the ground of there being conscience at all.

But what is this moral end, this principle to which all consciences *ought* to conform? What is it, when all things are taken into account, that is most desirable, most worthy to exist, or that has the chief *claim* upon our allegiance? Today, when we look back on the fundamentally different answers to these questions, and when we realize our own confusion about them, we wonder if there is any final answer to them at all, or whether they are childish and meaningless. Yet we must continue to ask them. And we cannot but hope that soon, even perhaps in your time, they may be finally answered in principle, though never in detail.

In Greece and Palestine two answers were made, and each a great one.

The Greeks, I suppose, may be said to have conceived the ideal of "the just man." They saw the difference between the private and the universal view, and they felt that to take account only of the needs of one's own body and oneself as a person against other persons was petty, arbitrary, incomplete, mean. The just man, they said in effect, is one who cares indeed for his own soul or personality, rather than for fleeting pleasures; but he cares most, not for himself, but for his city, for the community in which he is a member. And for his city he should care not merely as for a crowd of persons demanding pleasure, but as for an organized system in which each member has an allotted function and justification. And the supreme function, of which only the greatest individuals were capable, was said to be the pursuit of wisdom, the attempt to take all things into account at their true value, and so discover the good, and conduct oneself and rule others in accordance with that supreme knowledge.

Here indeed was a great answer to the question, and one which many have thought sufficient. But it was not final. It did not stress all that needed to be stressed even within the experience of that age. It was based on justice rather than on love. It began with the cultured individual's demand for self-increase and for harmony of mental content; and it passed on to the universal view only *because* this alone was found to afford personal fulfillment. The social life was to be pursued just *because* the citizen can find richer experience and activity than the man apart.

But with the coming of Christianity men found, not merely that justice was the way to self-fulfillment, but that their fellows were lovable. The extant form of society did not allow the fulfillment of every person; and it was obvious that many who were socially cramped were intrinsically no less worthy than many others who were favoured. Thus it was, perhaps, that the value of the individual experient became the basis of Christianity. And Christianity was also a revolt against an earlier moralism. It was recognized that each individual must seek, not merely to obey wise laws, but to embrace within the circle of his own felt needs the needs of his neighbours. This would seem to be the essence of the Christian ideal of the loving community. It was found to be involved in human nature itself that each man should "self-forgetfully" love others. Adapting an expression used in other connections by one of our philosophers I would say that the essence of Christianity is to have the needs of all other persons "ingredient" in oneself.

Why does the true Christian serve others? Not (I hope) just *because* to desert them would give *him* a pang. On the contrary the pang that he would have in deserting them springs from the prior fact that he recognizes their needs as indeed *their needs*. I would put it thus. Their needs are not motives of his conduct *because* he has taken possession of them, or conceived them on his own account within the womb of his own egoism. No, they are objectively needs whether he discovers them or not; and in his discovery of them *they* invade and possess *him*. His demand for their fulfillment is *their* demand through him. He is in part constituted by them.

But the Christian ideal, like those that preceded it, stressed certain values at the expense of others. Seeing the intrinsic good of every individual experient, it went on to assume that each individual must be eternal. For Christians have exaggerated the value of the individual experient "soul," even though their approach to such a view was not through self-love but love of others. They have insisted on the potential equality of individuals "in God's eyes," simply as being one and all centres of experience and will. They ignore all differences but differences in the capacity to love other experients, human and divine. They fixed man's attention on himself and the God which he made in his own likeness. They conceived a heaven in which individuals were to be fulfilled simply in an emotional attitude toward each other and their creator. The starry spheres were regarded but as a potter's wheel for the making of affectionate human beings, who in an after life should be perfected and compensated for their sufferings in this world.

You, looking back on my time with a certain aloofness, may smile when you learn that very many even of us are still enthralled so securely to the value of the experient ego, and so dismayed at the "injustice" of its fate on earth, that they cling to the belief in its immortality, claiming that if souls die the universe must be evil. And though even in your day you may not be entirely free from the primitive wish that your beloveds might live for ever, you must I think see with a clearness impossible to us that such cravings are foolish, if not immoral. For even I, blindly groping toward that wider view of existence which I trust you have attained, begin to understand that the experient soul, though indeed it is a great intrinsic good, is also but a tone in a more excellent music, which would be marred were its individual sounds not to follow one another into silence.

A good thing, indeed, is good eternally, however brief its existence. But continuance does not necessarily enhance its value. When we consider our dear ones in abstraction from the rest of the world, we cannot but desire immortality for them. But in those clear moments when we see the whole and are in love with it, we discover with sudden shame that to have demanded perpetuity even for the finest of human persons is as though a lover were to have gloated upon one gesture of the beloved, forgetting the swift soul. For in those clear moments persons are seen to be but gestures of the world, or foci kindled for a while with light from the stars.

But these moments perhaps lie.

LETTER III

Of worldliness and otherworldliness

Great Grandson,

My third letter must, like my second, temper the extravagance of my first. I spoke of a religion of worldliness; what, I wonder, did I really mean by that self-righteous devildom? You, who will perhaps never have suffered from that curious malady which has been called the non-conformist conscience, will easily detect in me an exaggerated dislike of piety, oddly mated with an itch to preach supreme values. This I suppose is the normal fate of the non-conformist mind when at last it has smelt the corruption of its own purity. It cannot break the habit of preaching and of pietism, so it merely orientates its pietism towards ends which formerly it would have condemned as wicked.

Help me with your imagined presence to think out this question of worldliness and unworldliness dispassionately.

The root of Christianity, I should say, was the apprehension of the beauty and loveableness of one's neighbours, and of their need. From love, more than from egoistic dread of extinction, sprang the doctrine of the immortal soul. But if all souls are precious, so is my own. And so a doctrine that began in love was often tripped into selfishness. Now the way to save the souls of others was to help them to transcend their petty selves and be absorbed emotionally into the life of the loving community whose true home was said to be eternity. To brood beyond the limits of petty interests, this was the way of salvation for one's neighbours, and for oneself. Thus a religion whose root was active love for men and women developed the ideal of otherworldliness, the aim of deserting all the misery and meanness of this planet by imaginative brooding on eternal verities. Love was first praised because it was the attitude appropriate to the objective loveliness of one's neighbours; but it came to be valued for its own sake, and to be the goal of all existence and the supreme excellence of God was even said to lie in his loving men *in spite* of their unworthiness to be loved. Love itself was the end, no matter what its object. This divorce of love from the loveliness of its object led easily to a subtle emotionalism according to which the effects of a man's conduct mattered less than "the state of his soul." Thus in a back-handed manner egotism of the subtlest kind received divine honours.

There is indeed an attitude sometimes confused with otherworldliness which is not egoistical. The truly religious consciousness might be described as a vague surmise that beyond the world of common sense, beyond the needs of our neighbours and the needs of the awakening social whole of mankind, lie higher cosmical needs which man cannot yet clearly apprehend though he must keep his heart open to feel them. And to this account of the religious spirit we should perhaps add the even vaguer sense that behind the apparent distinction of good and evil lies the truth that reality, just as it is, is perfect. Whether or not these obscure cognitions be true, this attitude of mind is a response as it were to a half-heard, half-imagined knocking at the outer doors of the personality; it is an enthusiastic readiness to adopt whatever in fact is the appropriate attitude to the real as a whole, but this should not be called otherworldliness, for it does not, like otherworldliness, despise and fear the world of everyday. It seeks only to know more of it and admire it more justly, and serve it more shrewdly.

Otherworldliness is quite different. It is a shameful desertion of the real, a willful deafness to all the urgent needs cognized in the world, and an attempt to satisfy one's own desire for pleasure and dread of pain by a system of fantasy. This treason has I think been fostered by an over-valuation of the mere processes of consciousness. For thus men came easily to think more of the good *will* than of the goodness of its goal, more of the artistic emotion than of the work of art, more of their consciences than of their neighbours, more of faith than of works.

But stay! The opposition of the ideals of faith and of works must not be so carelessly dismissed. Behind that bitter old controversy lie, I think, two truths that are simple and easily accepted, though their logical support is a complicated affair. It is true in the first place that the individual attains highest intrinsic excellence by opening his heart to those obscure intimations of cosmic value which are the essential religious experience. For in a sense the individual is greater and more self-complete the more the content of his experience approximates to the whole real. If then we are considering the individual alone, the external results of his conduct are irrelevant. *He* must be judged in terms of his own experience and will, not in terms of his external effects. And this is to judge him in terms of his "faith"; for we must certainly interpret "faith" to mean something more austere than a kind of blinkered and phthisic confidence.

But if we are considering the world at large, we must judge individuals in terms of their effect on the world. Even so, however, the last word is perhaps for faith rather than works. For the world on which the individual acts is, after all, other individuals; and the excellence of individuals, we have said, is in the breadth and truth of their mentality. Thus the goal of works is after all faith, broadly interpreted, but it is the faith of others. And it is faith, I should say, not as a mere emotional state to be enjoyed by a "soul," but in a sense very difficult to describe. The state of "faith" which each must seek to approach is, so to speak, the awakening of the universe to self-consciousness through the focalization of his percipient body. This state is excellent (if indeed it is excellent at all) because it is the world's fulfillment, not because it is the greatest joy a soul can have.

The ideal of good works began as a new sensitivity to the concrete needs of one's neighbours and a surmise as to cosmic needs; but subsequently it has often been adopted merely as a mechanical means toward private salvation. Thus once more was an outward-regarding precept adapted by egotism to its own uses. And in this service it was often turned from a concern for the effects of one's conduct to a mere thoughtless itch for activity, any activity socially approved, without serious criticism of the values served. Activity itself tended to seem its own justification.

Now the ideal of good works, when it is not merely a secret egoism, is essentially worldly, not otherworldly. It springs from admiration, love, and pity for members of this world for their own sake. It may be complicated by a surmise that each member is in some mysterious way the whole, and to be saved "for eternity," or for "another world." But primarily it is care for the member himself as he is seen to be in fact, here and now. It does not despise this world and shun it for another; it wants to make the best of this world, just because it is after all experienced as a world lovely though imperfect.

The attitude which is more conventionally called "worldliness" is a care for certain things in this world at the expense of others. It is a care for sensory pleasures and personal triumph, and when it loves, it admires in the beloved, and seeks to enhance in the beloved, only these minor goods. "Otherworldliness" is an excessive revulsion from these goods called worldly and a yearning for a world utterly different in which they have no part whatever. It is a kind of nausea brought on by an over-indulgence in things good in themselves but not the only good. Gorged to the point of vomiting we may long for a world in which food has no part whatever. Nauseated with the cruder values, we long for a sphere of "pure spirit," and seek to withdraw ourselves from this foundering world as rats from a sinking ship. This surely is the great treason. The advance from worldliness (in the conventional sense) is not to unworldliness but to a more thorough worldliness, a care not only for the cruder values revealed in this world but also for all its finer excellences which we foolishly supposed could constitute a world apart.

The "religion of worldliness" then is the will to know deeply the nature of this world, to understand good and evil, and to work for the fulfillment of this world's best capacities.

LETTER IV

Great Grandson,

I have introduced myself with a grand flourish, but what next? A second and a third letter I have already written and discarded, for they were still-born. I caught myself yawning when I read them over, yawning and hoping for the dinner bell. Clearly that is not the kind of letter I meant to write. I meant to make a direct and vivid confession of faith. I meant to distill the very essence of my life for you, the few drops of spirit that have flavoured my whole watery existence. It was to be caught in a little phial of crystal language and preserved for you (and then, I thought, I should be able to comfort myself even in my ceaseless futility with the certainty that one thing at least had been done well and serviceably). But all that came was second-hand truth in text-book jargon!

Is it all a delusion, then? Have I nothing to tell you? No, no, there is something that must be said; and if I don't say it, another will, damn him,—I mean thank God. But if there really is something to say, why don't I say it, and have done? I can't. And yet there the thing is; it won't leave me alone. It keeps nudging me at every turn, and looking me full in the face with the painful brightness of the sun, while seeming to say ironically, "Well, what about *me*? It's time you told them. I insist that everyone who has the pleasure of my acquaintance shall advertise me. Others are busy for me; but you?" In that bright moment it is all clear; but as soon as I get down to work there is nothing left but a sort of dazzlement and bewilderment, and an inarticulate echo of that gleam of the truth.

Such, you will say, is the fate of all mediocre minds when they over-reach their stature. It is as though there were some certain clear and exquisite percept which one were to encounter often but never remember, save as the hidden goal of a thousand "association paths" in the mind. If only one could be quit of the thing, or grasp it for ever!

There! I have it! There's a sparrow on the washhouse roof, and he's an angel of the Lord if ever there was one. He's sick, poor little devil. He's hunched in a tousled ball. He keeps blinking. Every now and then he pecks at his tummy. Now he has dropped a greenish-white mess behind him. That seems to have relieved him, for he is perking up somewhat. Now he's gone. Farewell, Sir! Good hunting! And good mating!

Well, and what of the sparrow? How, precisely, did he manage to illumine the situation? I do not claim to have seen in him mystically the very spirit of the Whole, or to have pierced intuitively beyond his shabby appearance to the perfect real of which he is an aspect. Such experiences are not for me, and therefore I suspect them. No, the little guttersnipe of the roof was a clear *symbol* of the Whole; but he no more *is* the Whole than "c a t" *is* pussy herself. He is far more than a symbol, and yet not the Whole. He is just himself, a very odd thing, which no one can intelligibly describe, though everyone (unsophisticated by theory) respects it as a bit of reality,—whatever that may mean.

Yes, he is a bit of reality, though not a very important bit. But stay! He *is* very important, for without him there would be a queer hole in the universe, and all things would be subtly disturbed. "Not a sparrow shall fall to the ground—." Moreover he is vastly important to himself; and what is the universal view but to take into account every private view? Not one of these curious self-importances (his and yours and mine and the rest) can be left out; but unfortunately they furiously conflict, and have somehow to be reconciled. And alas many of them are, in their very nature, irreconcilable. To embrace, they must first be dissolved and refashioned. Sparrow and cat,

German and Frenchman! (But in your time surely this last antithesis will have lost its point. Or is your Europe still mad with multiple personality?)

To return to the sparrow, what *is* he? A bundle of instincts and reflexes? What, I wonder, is that, unless it is a bundle of ways of behaving? And somehow what one *means* by "that sparrow" is not ways of behaving but something, however obscure, that does the behaving. Then is he perhaps a very complicated dance of electrons? Well, if that is what the little fellow is, electrons are very much more than the physicists mean by "electrons." Instincts may claim at least to be ways of psychical behaving, ways of knowing and striving and feeling; but electrons are but ways of physical behaving, ways of moving, in fact. Somehow or other, it seems, when the dance becomes sufficiently involved these ways of moving, which we call electrons, miraculously give birth to ways of knowing, striving and feeling. In the jargon of philosophers, the psychical "emerges" in a certain complexity of integration or organization of that which, in simpler patterns, is only physical.

But what *is* it that, organised in different patterns, behaves in different manners? Electrons, if they are more than ways of behaving, are clearly not little self-complete *things*. For some electrons somewhere in that sparrow are apparently much finer fellows than they could possibly be were they cast adrift. They are mysteriously given a richer nature by the form of their organization. They assume new ways of behaving. And further they as a whole are aware, they as a whole feel, they as a whole strive. They and their passerine pattern are, so to speak, mutually creative of each other. Each electron, we are told by one of our philosophers, "prehends" within itself all others, and is in turn itself "ingredient" in every other. Each one of them, without the society of the others organised in this passerine manner, would be something different through and through from what it is.

But the passerine form itself, which in a manner (we know not how) controls the sparrow's electrons, is in turn an expression of a certain environment, past and present. Ingredient in this sparrow are many features of my garden and all the careers of his ancestors. This little ball of flesh and feather is moulded from without just as each electron within it is moulded by the others.

Now there is one very striking respect in which the system of electrons in the sparrow differs from the system of the sparrow and its environment. In the system of the sparrow's electrons the passerine form itself seems to bring into being new kinds of activity biological and psychological. But the system of the sparrow and its environment is not itself a biological or psychological unit, behaving as a single whole. Always it is the sparrow that behaves biologically and psychologically, not the stone on which it perches.

In a stone there are electrons, and each prehends all the others, and the rest of the universe; but the stone is no biological unity.

In a society of human persons (as I see it) there is no biological unity, though it is composed of biological individuals, and each individual is what he is by virtue of his social environment. Society itself does not behave; its members do.

The stone is a crowd of very simple beings, each of which is indeed an expression of the others and of all else in the world, but is not dominated by any unity of the stone. The sparrow is multitudinous "clay" organised into one life. A man is another such but far richer and more unitary; for he acts in relation to things inconceivable to a sparrow, and he brings to bear upon each situation far wider regions of the past. A society of men is, like a stone, a crowd of beings, but of biological beings.

NOTES

1. Many of these very early letters to and from William Clibbett Stapledon still survive and are in the private collection of John D. Stapledon.
2. Olaf Stapledon to Agnes Miller, 4 June 1914, in *Talking Across the World*, 41.
3. Olaf Stapledon to Agnes Miller, 5 February 1912. Collection of John D. Stapledon.
4. Olaf Stapledon to Agnes Miller, 10 May 1911. Collection of John D. Stapledon.
5. About the first project Stapledon wrote that the letters "should be the best of the book." Clearly alluding to his own correspondence, he said that for the second project "I have no end of valuable material." Olaf Stapledon to Agnes Miller, 13 January 1916 and 9 May 1916. Collection of John D. Stapledon.
6. Enclosure in letter of Olaf Stapledon to Agnes Miller, 2 June 1917, in *Talking Across the World*, 228.
7. "Problems and Solutions, or the Future."
8. "Revolt Against Death," 97.
9. See, for instance, on atomic power "Our Stupendous Future" and "Social Implications of Atomic Power." For his many short pieces on issues of war and peace in 1948–1949 see items C176–77, C180–83, C188–89 in Satty and Smith.
10. "The Peak and the Town" was printed for the first time in the front matter of Satty and Smith, xxvii–xxxviii.
11. "Areopagitica" in *Complete Poems and Major Prose of John Milton*, 720.
12. The small manuscript pages of the work titled, at first, *A Letter to the Future* and, later, *Letters to the Future*, are in the Stapledon Archive at the University of Liverpool. The pages are not dated, but apparent references to the atomic bomb in the manuscript suggest that the writing was done in the last five years of Stapledon's life, between 1945 and 1950. The transcription from the manuscript published below is by permission of the Librarian, Sydney Jones Library, University of Liverpool, and the estate of Olaf Stapledon.

WORKS CITED

Milton, John. "Areopagitica." In *Complete Poems and Major Prose of John Milton*, ed. Merritt Y. Hughes. New York: Odyssey Press, 1957.

Satty, Harvey J., and Curtis C. Smith. *Olaf Stapledon: A Bibliography*. Westport, Conn.: Greenwood Press, 1984.

Stapledon, Olaf. "Our Stupendous Future." *The Leader* (18 August 1945): 9, 22.

———. "Problems and Solutions, or the Future." In *An Outline for Boys and Girls and Their Parents*, edited by Naomi Mitchison. London: Victor Gollancz, 1932.

———. "Revolt Against Death." In *Poets of Merseyside: An Anthology of Present-Day Liverpool Poetry*, edited by S. Fowler Wright. London: Merton Press, 1923.

———. "Social Implications of Atomic Power." *The Norseman* 3 (November-December 1945): 390–93.

———. *Talking Across the World: The Love Letters of Olaf Stapledon and Agnes Miller, 1913–1919*, edited by Robert Crossley. Hanover, NH: University Press of New England, 1987.

———. Unpublished letters in the collection of John D. Stapleton.

Bibliography

This is a selective bibliography. The list of secondary sources excludes reviews of Stapledon's books, brief reference articles, and books that do not have chapters devoted exclusively to Stapledon. For an exhaustive list of primary sources, see Harvey J. Satty and Curtis C. Smith, *Olaf Stapledon: A Bibliography*.

The editors wish to acknowledge the valuable advice of Robert Crossley and Curtis C. Smith in the preparation of this bibliography

PRIMARY SOURCES

Fiction

"The Seed and the Flower." *Friends' Quarterly Examiner* 50 (October 1916): 464–75. [Short story]

Last and First Men: A Story of the Near and Far Future. London: Methuen, 1930.

Last Men in London. London: Methuen, 1932.

Odd John: A Story Between Jest and Earnest. London: Methuen, 1935.

Star Maker. London: Methuen, 1937.

Darkness and the Light. London: Methuen, 1942.

Old Man in New World. London: Allen & Unwin, P.E.N. Books, 1944.

Sirius: A Fantasy of Love and Discord. London: Secker & Warburg, 1944.

Death into Life. London: Methuen, 1946.

The Flames: A Fantasy. London: Secker & Warburg, 1947.

A Man Divided. London: Methuen, 1950.

The Opening of the Eyes, ed. Agnes Z. Stapledon. London: Methuen, 1954.

4 Encounters. Hayes, Middlesex: Bran's Head Books, 1976.

"Nebula Maker." Hayes, Middlesex: Bran's Head Books, 1976.

Far Future Calling: Uncollected Science Fiction and Fantasies of Olaf Stapledon, ed. Sam Moskowitz. Philadelphia: Oswald Train, 1979. [Includes, by Stapledon, the short stories "The Man Who Became a Tree," "A Modern Magician," "East Is West," "Arms out of Hand," and "A World of Sound"; the radio play *Far Future Calling*; and the reprinted essay "Interplanetary Man"; also includes contributions by Sam Moskowitz and Harvey Satty.]

"The Peak and the Town." In *Olaf Stapledon: A Bibliography*, ed. Harvey J. Satty and Curtis C. Smith. Westport, Conn.: Greenwood Press, 1984; pp. xxvii–xxxviii. [Short story]

Poems

Latter-Day Psalms. Liverpool: Henry Young & Sons, 1914.

"God the Artist," "Creator Creatus," "A Prophet's Tragedy," "The Good," "Revolt Against Death," "The Unknown," "Futility," and "The Relativity of Beauty." In *Poets of Merseyside: An Anthology of Present-Day Liverpool Poetry*, ed. S. Fowler Wright. London: Merton Press, 1923; pp. 93–100.

"Pain," "Swallows at Maffrecourt," "Moriturus," "A Prophet's Tragedy," "God the Artist." In *Voices on the Wind*, second series, ed. S. Fowler Wright. London: Merton Press, 1924; pp. 165–67.

Non-fiction (Books and Pamphlets)

A Modern Theory of Ethics: A Study of the Relations of Ethics and Psychology. London: Methuen, 1929.

Waking World. London: Methuen, 1934.

Saints and Revolutionaries. London: William Heinemann, 1939.

New Hope for Britain. London: Methuen, 1939.

Philosophy and Living. 2 volumes. Harmondsworth, Middlesex: Penguin, 1939.

Beyond the "Isms." [Searchlight Books, No. 16] London: Secker & Warburg, 1942.

Seven Pillars of Peace. London: Common Wealth [*sic*] Popular Library, 1946.

Youth and Tomorrow. London: St. Botolph, 1946.

Letters

"The Correspondence of Olaf Stapledon and H. G. Wells, 1931–1942," ed. Robert Crossley. In *Science Fiction Dialogues*, ed. Gary Wolfe. Chicago: Academy Chicago, 1982; pp. 27–57.

Talking Across the World: The Love Letters of Olaf Stapledon and Agnes Miller, 1913–1919, ed. Robert Crossley. Hanover, N.H., and London: University Press of New England, 1987.

[See also Mitchison under Secondary Sources]

Selected Essays

"The Splendid Race." *The Old Abbotsholmian* 2 (1907): 159–61.

"The Novice Schoolmaster." *The Old Abbotsholmian* 3 (1910): 14–18.

"Poetry and the Worker." *The Highway* 6 (October 1913): 4–6.

"The Reflections of an Ambulance Orderly." *The Friend* (14 April 1916): 246.

"Rhyme, Assonance and Vowel Contrast." *Poetry* 7 (August–September 1924): 194–96.

"A Theory of the Unconscious." *Monist* 37 (July 1927): 422–44.

"The Location of Physical Objects." *Journal of Philosophical Studies* 4 (January 1929): 64–75.

"The Remaking of Man." *The Listener* 5 (8 April 1931): 575–76.

"Problems and Solutions, or the Future." In *An Outline for Boys & Girls and Their Parents*, ed. Naomi Mitchison. London: Victor Gollancz, 1932; pp. 691–749.

"Education and World Citizenship." In *Manifesto: Being the Book of the Federation of Progressive Societies and Individuals*, ed. C. E. M. Joad. London: Allen & Unwin, 1934; pp. 142–63.

"Experiences in the Friends' Ambulance Unit." In *We Did Not Fight: 1914–18 Experiences of War Resisters*, ed. Julian Bell. London: Cobden-Sanderson, 1935; pp. 359–74.

"Science, Art and Society." *The London Mercury* 38 (October 1938): 521–28.

"Writers and Politics." *Scrutiny* 8 (September 1939): 151–56.

"Escapism in Literature." *Scrutiny* 8 (December 1939): 298–308.

"Federalism and Socialism." In *Federal Union: A Symposium*, ed. M. Chaning-Pearce. London: Jonathan Cape, 1940; pp. 115–29.

"Tradition and Innovation to-Day." *Scrutiny* 9 (June 1940): 33–45.

"Literature and the Unity of Man." In *Writers in Freedom: A Symposium*, ed. Herman Ould. London: Hutchinson, [1942]; pp. 113–19.

"Sketch-Map of Human Nature." *Philosophy* 17 (July 1942): 210–30.

"Morality, Scepticism, and Theism." *Proceedings of the Aristotelian Society*, n.s., 44 (1943–44): 15–42.

"The Great Certainty." In *In Search of Faith: A Symposium*, ed. Ernest W. Martin. London: Lindsey Drummond, 1944; pp. 37–59.

"What *Are* 'Spiritual' Values?" In *Freedom of Expression: A Symposium*, ed. Herman Ould. London: Hutchinson, 1944; pp. 16–26.

"Our Stupendous Future." *Leader* 2, no. 44 (18 August 1945): 9, 22.

"Man: Should We Re-Make Him?" *Leader* 2 (1 September 1945): 12–13.

"Planning and Liberty: Talks with the Troops." *The London Quarterly of World Affairs* 11 (October 1945): 245–53.

"Social Implications of Atomic Power." *The Norseman* 3 (November–December 1945): 390–93.

"Education for Personality-in-Community." *New Era in Home and School* 27 (March 1946): 63–67.

"The Religious Approach." In *The Present Question*, ed. H. Westmann. London: Chapman & Hall, 1947; pp. 108–23.

"Data for a World View: 1. The Human Situation and Natural Science." *Enquiry* [1] (April 1948): 13–18.

"Data for a World View: 2. Paranormal Experiences." *Enquiry* 1 ([May 1948]): 13–18.

"Interplanetary Man?" *Journal of the British Interplanetary Society* 7 (November 1948): 213–33. Reprinted in *Far Future Calling: Uncollected Science Fiction and Fantasies of Olaf Stapledon*, pp. 209–52.

"Personality and Liberty." *Philosophy* 24 (April 1949): 144–56.

"Ethical Values Common to East and West" and "From England." In *Speaking of Peace*, ed. Daniel S. Gillmor. New York: National Council of the Arts, Sciences and Professions, 1949; pp. 119–21, 130–31.

"A Plain Man Talks About Values." *Rider's Review* 76 (Spring 1950): 22–28.

"The Bridge Between [Marxist Values and Christian Values]." In *Two Worlds in Focus: Studies of the Cold War*. London: National Peace Council, 1950; pp. 44–60.

Unpublished Materials

A large collection of unpublished materials by Stapledon forms the Olaf Stapledon Archive at the Sydney Jones Library, University of Liverpool. Materials in the archive include complete holograph book manuscripts; manuscripts and typescripts for books, book chapters, articles, poems, and stories; proofs for books and articles; manuscript notes; appointment books and diaries; lecture notes; correspondence; Stapledon's scrapbooks; and Stapledon's Ph.D. dissertation, entitled "Meaning." The H. G. Wells Collection at the University of Illinois at Urbana-Champaign includes twenty-six letters from Stapledon to Wells, and there is an extensive collection of letters from Stapledon to J. B. Priestley, Herman Ould, and others at the Humanities Research Center, University of Texas at Austin. Other materials, including the largest collection of letters to and from Stapledon, are in the possession of his son, Mr. John David Stapledon of Heswall, Wirral, Merseyside.

SECONDARY SOURCES

Aldiss, Brian W. "Foreword" to *Star Maker*. Los Angeles: Jeremy P. Tarcher, 1987; pp. ix-xiv.

Bailey, K. V. "A Prized Harmony: Myth, Symbol and Dialectic in the Novels of Olaf Stapledon." *Foundation* 15 (January 1979): 53–66.

Bengels, Barbara. "Olaf Stapledon's 'Odd John' and 'Sirius': Ascent into Bestiality." *Foundation* 9 (November 1975): 57–61.

Benford, Gregory. "Foreword" to *Last and First Men*. Los Angeles: Jeremy P. Tarcher, 1988; pp. ix-xii.

Branham, Robert. "Stapledon's 'Agnostic Mysticism.'" *Science-Fiction Studies* 9 (November 1982): 249–56.

Brunet, Roger Andrew. "The Mystic Vision of Olaf Stapledon: The Spirit in Crisis." M.A. Thesis, Carleton University (Ottawa), 1968.

Campbell, James L., Sr. "Olaf Stapledon, 1886–1950." In *Science Fiction Writers: Critical Studies of the Major Authors from the Early Nineteenth Century to the Present Day*, ed. E. F. Bleiler. New York: Charles Scribner's Sons, 1982; pp. 91–100.

Casillo, Robert. "Olaf Stapledon and John Ruskin." *Science-Fiction Studies* 9 (November 1982): 306–21.

Clark, Stephen R. L. "Olaf Stapledon: Philosopher and Fabulist." *Chronicles* 10 (December 1986): 14–16, 18.

Coates, J. B. "Olaf Stapledon." In *Ten Modern Prophets*. London: Frederick Muller, 1944; pp. 151–66.

Crossley, Robert. "Famous Mythical Beasts: Olaf Stapledon and H. G. Wells." *Georgia Review* 36 (Fall 1982): 619–35.

———. "Politics and the Artist: The Aesthetic of *Darkness and the Light*." *Science-Fiction Studies* 9 (November 1982): 294–305.

———. "Olaf Stapledon and the Idea of Science Fiction." *Modern Fiction Studies* 32 (Spring 1986): 21–42.

———. "Introduction." In *Talking Across the World: The Love Letters of Olaf Stapledon and Agnes Miller, 1913–1919*. Hanover, N.H., and London: University Press of New England, 1987; pp. xi-xii.

Davenport, Basil. "The Vision of Olaf Stapledon." Introduction to *To the End of Time: The Best of Olaf Stapledon*. New York: Funk & Wagnalls, 1953; pp. vii-xix.

Elkins, Charles. "The Worlds of Olaf Stapledon: Myth or Fiction?"*Mosaic* 13 (Spring/Summer 1980): 145–52.

Fiedler, Leslie A. *Olaf Stapledon: A Man Divided*. New York: Oxford University Press, 1983.

Glicksohn, Susan. "A City of Which the Stars Are Suburbs." In *SF: The Other Side of Realism*, ed. Thomas D. Clareson. Bowling Green, Ohio: Bowling Green University Popular Press, 1971; pp. 334–47.

Goodheart, Eugene. "Olaf Stapledon's *Last and First Men*." In *No Place Else: Explorations in Utopian and Dystopian Fiction*, ed. Eric S. Rabkin, Martin H. Greenberg, and Joseph D. Olander. Carbondale: Southern Illinois University Press, 1983; pp. 78–93.

Huntington, John. "Olaf Stapledon and the Novel about the Future." *Contemporary Literature* 22 (Summer 1981): 349–65.

———. "Remembrance of Things to Come: Narrative Technique in *Last and First Men*." *Science-Fiction Studies* 9 (November 1982): 257–64.

Kinnaird, John. "Olaf Stapledon." In *Twentieth-Century Science Fiction Writers*, ed. Curtis C. Smith. New York: St. Martin's Press, 1981.

———. *Olaf Stapledon*. Mercer Island, Wash.: Starmont House, 1986.

Lavabre, Simone. "Un utopiste au XXe siècle, W. Olaf Stapledon." *Caliban* 2 (1967): 249–66.

Lem, Stanislaw. "On Stapledon's *Last and First Men*," trans. Istvan Csicsery-Ronay, Jr. *Science-Fiction Studies* 13 (November 1986): 272–91.

———. "On Stapledon's *Star Maker*," Trans. Istavan Csicsery-Ronay, Jr. *Science Fiction Studies* 14 (March 1987): 1–8.

Lessing, Doris. "Afterword" to *Last and First Men*. Los Angeles: Jeremy P. Tarcher, 1988; pp. 305–307.

Martin, E. W. "Between the Devil and the Deep Sea: The Philosophy of Olaf Stapledon." In *The Pleasure Ground: A Miscellany of English Writing*, ed. Malcolm Elwin. London: MacDonald, 1947; pp. 204–16.

McCarthy, Patrick A. *Olaf Stapledon*. Boston: Twayne Publishers, 1982.

———. "Olaf Stapledon." In *British Novelists 1930–1959*, ed. Bernard Oldsey. Detroit: Gale Research, 1983; pp. 508–14.

———. "*Last and First Men* as Miltonic Epic." *Science-Fiction Studies* 11 (November 1984): 244–52.

Michel, John B. "The Philosophical Novels of Olaf Stapledon: Studies in a New Type of Outlook." *The Alchemist* 1 (Summer 1940): 7–15.

Mitchison, Naomi. "Star Maker." In *You May Well Ask: A Memoir 1920–1940*. London: Victor Gollancz, 1979; pp. 138–42.

Moskowitz, Sam. "Olaf Stapledon: Cosmic Philosopher." In *Explorers of the Infinite: Shapers of Science Fiction*. Cleveland: World Publishing Co., 1963; pp. 261–77. Reprinted in *Darkness and the Light*. Westport, Conn.: Hyperion Press, 1974.

———. "Olaf Stapledon: The Man Behind the Works." *Fantasy Commentator* 4 (Winter 1978–79): 3–26, 32–33. Reprinted in *Far Future Calling: Uncollected Science Fiction and Fantasies of Olaf Stapledon*; pp. 15–69.

———. "Peace and Olaf Stapledon." *Fantasy Commentator* 4 (Winter 1979–80): 72–81. Reprinted in *Far Future Calling: Uncollected Science Fiction and Fantasies of Olaf Stapledon*; pp. 253–75.

———. "Olaf Stapledon: His Son, His Daughter, His Political Perceptions." *Fantasy Commentator* 5 (Fall 1985): 151–62, 175.

Rabkin, Eric. "The Composite Fiction of Olaf Stapledon." *Science-Fiction Studies* 9 (November 1982): 238–48.

Rutledge, Amelia A. "*Star Maker*: The Agnostic Quest." *Science-Fiction Studies* 9 (November 1982): 274–83.

Satty, Harvey J., and Curtis C. Smith. "Introduction" to *Last Men in London*. Boston: G. K. Hall, 1975; pp. v–xiv.

———. *Olaf Stapledon: A Bibliography*. Westport, Conn.: Greenwood Press, 1984.

Shelton, Robert. "The Mars-Begotten Men of Olaf Stapledon and H. G. Wells." *Science-Fiction Studies* 11 (March 1984): 1–14.

Smith, Curtis C. "Olaf Stapledon: Saint and Revolutionary." *Extrapolation* 13 (December 1971): 5–15.

———. "Introduction" to *To the End of Time: The Best of Olaf Stapledon*. Boston: Gregg Press, 1975; pp. v–xi.

———. "Olaf Stapledon's Dispassionate Objectivity." In *Voices for the Future: Essays on Major Science Fiction Writers*, ed. Thomas D. Clareson. Bowling Green, Ohio: Bowling Green University Popular Press, 1976; pp. 44–63.

———. "The Manuscript of *Last and First Men*: Towards a Variorum." *Science-Fiction Studies* 9 (November 1982): 265–73.

———. "Horror Versus Tragedy: Mary Shelley's *Frankenstein* and Olaf Stapledon's *Sirius*." *Extrapolation* 26 (Spring 1985): 66–73.

———. "Olaf Stapledon and the Immortal Spirit." In *Death and the Serpent: Immortality in Science Fiction and Fantasy*, ed. Carl B. Yoke and Donald M. Hassler. Westport, Conn.: Greenwood Press, 1985; pp. 103–13.

Swanson, Roy Arthur. "The Spiritual Factor in *Odd John* and *Sirius*." *Science-Fiction Studies* 9 (November 1982): 284–93.

Tremaine, Louis. "Olaf Stapledon's Note on Magnitude." *Extrapolation* 23 (Fall 1982): 243–53.

———. "Historical Consciousness in Stapledon and Malraux." *Science-Fiction Studies* 11 (July 1984): 130–38.

Index

About the Contributors

ROBERT CROSSLEY, whose articles cover subjects ranging from Pope's *Iliad* to J. R. R. Tolkien and Sylvia Townsend Warner, is the author of *H. G. Wells* (Starmont Reader's Guide series) and editor of *Talking Across the World: The Love Letters of Olaf Stapledon and Agnes Miller, 1913–1919*. His current project is the biography of Olaf Stapledon. At the University of Massachusetts at Boston, where he is Professor of English, he has won awards for teaching, service, and scholarship.

CHARLES ELKINS is Professor of English and Vice Provost for Academic Affairs at Florida International University in Miami. He is co-editor of *Science-Fiction Studies* and has published several articles on science fiction writers, including Olaf Stapledon.

MARTIN H. GREENBERG is Professor of Political Science and Literature at the University of Wisconsin–Green Bay. He has co-authored or co-edited more than a dozen books on science fiction, including the award-winning *Science Fiction and Fantasy Series and Sequels* (1986). He is also co-editor of the Alternatives series of books about science fiction at Southern Illinois University Press.

CHERYL HERR, an Associate Professor of English at the University of Iowa, has written *Joyce's Anatomy of Culture* and numerous articles. She is now at work on a cycle of essays about spatial organization in Irish culture and is completing an edition of previously unpublished Irish political melodramas.

PATRICK A. McCARTHY is Professor of English and director of the English graduate program at the University of Miami. He is the author of *The Riddles of Finnegans Wake*, *Olaf Stapledon*, and many articles on modern literature, and editor of *Critical Essays on Samuel Beckett*. At present he is writing a book on Joyce's *Ulysses*.

ROBERT SHELTON teaches English and expository writing at Oberlin College. He has written on H. G. Wells, Olaf Stapledon, Arthur C. Clarke, and Doris Lessing, as well as topics in film studies, rhetoric, and medicine and humanities.

CURTIS C. SMITH is Professor of Humanities at the University of Houston–Clear Lake. He is a pioneering Stapledon scholar and the editor of *Twentieth-Century Science Fiction Writers*. Currently he is finishing *A Reader's Guide to Mack Reynolds*.

LOUIS TREMAINE, who teaches English and comparative literature at the University of Richmond, has published articles on Olaf Stapledon in *Extrapolation* and *Science-Fiction Studies*. His other research interests include African and modern Afro-American literature. He is presently at work on a study of the use of literature in cross-cultural interpretation.